A SNITCH ON TIME

An Original Story
With Real-Life Incidents
By
PROLIFIC, INTERNATIONAL BESTSELLING
AUTHOR

JOHN A. ANDREWS

CREATOR OF
RENEGADE COPS
THE RUDE BUAY SERIES
&
THE WHODUNIT CHRONICLES
CO - AUTHOR OF
THE MACOS ADVENTURE II – THE AUTHORITY SQUAD

08/10/18

A SNITCH ON TIME

Published in the U.S.A. by
Books That Will Enhance Your Life

A L I
Andrews Leadership International
www.JohnAAndrews.com

ISBN: 978-0-9848980-8-4
Cover Design: ALI
Edited by: ALI

THE WHODUNIT CHRONICLES II

A SNITCH ON TIME

TABLE OF CONTENTS

A SNITCH ON TIME

THE CRASH
THE SHOOTING
THE UNCANNY WITNESS

A NOVEL BASED ON BLACK TEEN KILLINGS BY COPS.

A BLACK TEEN IS GUNNED DOWN BY VETERAN NYPD OFFICER ELI WALSH IMMEDIATELY AFTER A TRAFFIC ACCIDENT INVOLVING HIS BMW AND THE OFFICER'S CRUISER. WALSH CLAIMED HE SHOT THE 19-YEAR-OLD IN SELF-DEFENSE. BUT THE TEEN'S PARENTS WOULDN'T LEAVE ANY STONE UNTURNED IN ORDER TO FIND JUSTICE.

CHAPTER 1

The shadows lengthen across the strip mall parking lot in Floral Park, Queens, New York. Not far from Jamaica, NY, a small suburban community just a few miles west of Long Island. The fiery backdrop of the sunset lends its dwindling presence. The music fades at the neighborhood block party. Traffic thins out before bottlenecking in front of the mini-mall, landmarked by an oversized Seven Eleven convenient store.

Patrons crowd into the store to grab a smoothie drink or stock up on drinks for their intended party after the party.

Michael James, a 19-year-old African-American teenager pulls up in his mint conditioned, fully loaded, 900 Series, black on black crisp BMW.

Striding to her black, late edition Porsche is Tacoma Stanley. She is tall, slender, and dark skinned with long black hair, lips, and a curvaceous body to die for. Tacoma is drinking a multi-colored smoothie with the aid of a red, white and blue straw.

Michael rolls down the passenger window and *hollas* at the *Magnet*. She pretends she doesn't see or hear him.

Meanwhile, a less chic automobile: a Ford Mustang speeds away from the parking lot.

Michael's car advances as if to cut off Tacoma before she gets in and disappears. Tacoma is about to enter through the driver's door.

A fast speeding, no lights flashing NYPD cruiser leaving the parking lot, crashes into Michael's BMW in an unavoidable collision. It barely missed sideswiping Tacoma's Porsche.

Michael is shaken up but unhurt. He jumps out to investigate the damage.

A SNITCH ON TIME

"Retard! You crashed my ride. What's the matter with you?"
Says Michael.
NYPD officer, Eli Walsh pushes the ejected airbag out of the way. His lips move as if uttering some choice words to the teen. He steps out from under the driver's wheel and shoots Michael James point blank in the chest. Michael falls to the ground and bleeding from that chest wound.
In the meantime, Walsh's partner in crime officer Marcus Fenton sitting on the front passenger seat is hurt. He is bleeding from a concussion suffered as he collided with the cruiser's roof. His airbag chose not to activate.
Tacoma, who witnessed the scene unfolds from her vantage point, yells out:
"Murder in the second degree! That's what you-all do. Kill black men or put them in jail. This has to stop."
Officer Walsh responds,
"Shut up bitch! I could have you arrested for prostitution."
"I'll sue your ass. I am a virgin; never been touched by any man. You wanna mess with me? Or you want to shoot me too? Go ahead shoot me, you punk, rookie. If you were gun-less I'd take you down."
Responds Tacoma in a peeved manner.

A SNITCH ON TIME

Before Walsh could complete a distress call to 911, paramedics and NYPD vehicles have already encamped onto the crime scene.
In the meantime, Tacoma's iPhone's video recorder is working overtime on top of her car's dashboard.
Medics, drag Officer Fenton onto a gurney and into an awaiting ambulance.
Michael James is searched for weapons but possesses none. Still maintaining a pulse he's placed in an ambulance and whisked away to the nearby Queens Hospital.
Officer Walsh is questioned and driven away in another NYPD cruiser.
Detective Sam Black, a veteran with the NYPD and Pete Malcolm a rookie gleaned evidence from the crime scene. Additionally, two detectives Claude Mason of senior years and Maria Vasquez in her early 30s question witness Tacoma Stanley.
In the meantime, other NYPD officers secure the crime scene with yellow tape.
"Another black teen got shot!"
States the Seven Eleven Middle Eastern store manager Abdullah Sadiek, who is now standing at the store's front entrance - stunned.
Bystanders, even though they weren't present at the time of the shooting or the crash vent their displeasure

with the NYPD and other law enforcement entities across the country.

CHAPTER 2

With the crime scene already secured and yellow taped, two NYPD cruisers idly wait on the side of the street next to the mini mall. Their presences serve both as a deterrent as well as a sense of enforcement.

By this time, the news of the shooting tragedy had been widespread, and many observers came to see what

they had missed. Many of them had already formed their own opinion of what really went down.
"They keep killing off our young people." One Caucasian Middle-aged woman exclaimed.
You see; it was not the first time that a black teen was shot by a cop. It was just over a year ago; sixteen-year-old Kimani Gray was shot multiple times by two NYPD officers in the neighboring borough of Brooklyn. That incident led to rioting in his East Flatbush neighborhood until a curfew brought some calm.
A year before that, the 17-year-old Trayvon Martin from Miami Gardens, Florida was shot by Officer George Zimmerman. In that trial, the Officer walked scot free.

MEANWHILE, OUTSIDE THE QUEENS HOSPITAL, a growing crowd assembles. Police barricade already in place to keep the remaining visitors as well as their love symbols at bay. Earlier visitors brought Michael flowers, cards, as well as other sentiments.
In the front of the line, most of the girls, his age planted themselves. Tacoma stands out. She spits the song "It's all about his *Beema*" as an NYPD officer gait while he surveys the flustered crowd. Her friends joined in on the chorus.

A SNITCH ON TIME

Inside the hospital, a room was previously prepared for the injured Michael. His room was so far filled with cards and other get well sentiments, brought by the earlier visitors. The room looked like a decorated Christmas tree. There was so much *we love you* Michael's tokens that they had to turn off the surplus. Some cards even though signed: *Michael we love you* were given away to strangers whom he never met.

A SNITCH ON TIME

CHAPTER 3

Inside the E.R. Michael's Mom and Dad, Lawrence and Odessa James waited unnerved as doctors worked hard to keep Michael alive. His parents watched the monitor as it displayed irregular highs and lows. Suddenly, the positive reading ceased.

The chief attending physician, Dr. Preet Ellis, an East Indian woman in her mid-30s exclaimed:

A SNITCH ON TIME

"He didn't make it!"
Odessa, holding onto Lawrence in tears, pleads:
"Is that all you can do, doctor?"
"Mrs. James, it's a miracle your son did not die on the spot. That bullet ruptured his aorta. I have no idea what kept him alive for so long?"
"So how about… the iron, that shocking instrument... defibrillator? You can try that can't you?"
Dr. Ellis shakes her head,
"No."
Is that all doctor?" continues Odessa.
"Prayer,"
Says Dr. Ellis.
"We already did."
Replies Lawrence.
"Accept my condolences. I have two twin boys. They turn 19 on Saturday."
Says Dr. Ellis.
Michael's parents comfort each other in tears. Reality finally sinks in. They're firstborn after 19 years was dead.

THE NEWS OF MICHAEL'S DEATH traveled speedily: First to the crowd of over 100 well-wishers waiting outside the Hospital's entrance. Many who were still holding on to sentiments used them to decorate the blue and white police barricades. The new arrivals in the crowd displayed placards reading:

1. Racial Injustice.
2. Shoot First Ask Questions Later Must Be Outlawed.
3. Stop Killing Our Teens.
4. Courtesy.
5. Professionalism.
6. Respect.

Radio and TV stations were running the news monotonously. Multiple news crews assembled and broadcast from outside the hospital grounds. Twitter became flooded with tweets concerning the tragedy. Facebook posts escalated. The whole social media arena was slammed. Pictures of the crime scene and Michael's photos plastered Tumblr as well as Instagram.

IN THAT SAME HOSPITAL, though, in another room, NYPD Officer Marcus Fenton lay in bed not only with a bandaged head but with intravenous attachments to his body. It was reported by the Medical Staff that he lost so much blood; they feared he might end up brain dead.

Inside the lobby, many NYPD Officers provided security for their fellow officer. Some were armed with semi-automatic weapons. Many of them no doubt wondered if Fenton was going to be next. This opportunity gave them a chance to show genuine CPR - Courtesy, Professionalism, and Respect.

A SNITCH ON TIME

CHAPTER 4

The black teen Kimani Gray, shot in Brooklyn last spring, as well as the acquittal of George Zimmerman who shot the Trayvon Martin in Florida were still fresh in the air. The teenagers in Michael James' Queens, New York neighborhood decided they are going to let their voice be heard and presence felt. They took to the streets; looting, vandalizing and most of all ready to lay down their lives.

Many teens armed themselves with baseball bats, which they utilized to shatter store display windows as well as supermarket glass doors. Some took away merchandise while others vandalized to vent their frustrations with the NYPD for killing off their peers.

Five teens broke into a village supermarket and were immediately arrested by police. One of them yelled out while getting handcuffed.

"Please don't arrest me. I can't let my parents know I did this."

On another block, it seemed as if the revolution had already begun. Some teens demonstrated with signs reading: The Killing of Our Youths Must Stop.

We Are The Future.

Shoot First Ask Questions Later Should Be A Crime.

The violence escalated as many teens lay down in streets disrupting the flow of traffic.

It wasn't long before additional NYPD Officers moved in, mounted, in cruisers, buses, motorbikes and aerially by helicopter. Using teargas as well as military gear, they could restrain the disruptive youths. Many of them were handcuffed and placed on NYPD Buses headed for the nearby police precinct.

A SNITCH ON TIME

The news media soon became inundated covering the major fiasco which had resulted from the shooting death of Michael James by NYPD Officer Eli Walsh.

CHAPTER 5

Further up to the street where the shooting took place, a candlelight vigil was underway. Many Church members, other friends as well as some of the teen's family brought candles, flowers, and cards. Odessa James, Michaels' Mom and her 16-year-old son Jason James hang a sign displaying a portrait of Michael at Church playing the piano, above it R.I.P in big bold letters.

A SNITCH ON TIME

Meanwhile, in front of the Seven-Eleven Lawrence James, Michaels' Dad, a clergy at the local Presbyterian Church clusters with Abdullah Sadeik and immediately draws a crowd.

"Michael grew up in our Church and played the organ and piano like no one we've ever had."

Says his Dad.

"He was getting ready to join the naval forces in a few months. He wanted to be involved in another cause greater than himself. He wanted to fight for his country when that opportunity presented itself."

His Dad continues.

Odessa James after conversing with some passersby joins the huddle holding on tightly to Jason's hand and drying her weeping eyes. Catching on to her husband's dialog, she chimes in.

"When he played that piano and organ you could feel the Holy Spirit move inside the Church."

She dries more tears from both of her cheeks and continues:

"They had no right to shoot him. He was not even a violent kid. I can see him being upset about his Beema. I would be too if someone crashed my brand-new automobile after two days of purchase. He had been saving for three years to buy that car."

Abdullah, glancing over at the crime scene and the two parked police cars, back at Michael's parents and more

so at their 16-year-old son, responds: "He might have survived if he was not shot in the heart. He was a regular customer who always picked up a Raspberry Ice Tea and a pack of Tic Tacs."
Someone inside the store yells:
"Manager!"
Abdullah says:
"My condolences,"
He returns inside to his post behind the cash register. The checkout line grows. The huddle outside the store shrinks as many mourners disperse.
It wasn't long before an NYPD van patrolled the area with the use of a public address system. The warning was repeated continuously:
"Get off the streets if you are 20 years old and under, or you could get arrested. You must be off the streets by 9:00 PM." Many at the vigil heard about the prior arrests. Lawrence and Odessa huddled with elderly couple glances over and notices the sad look on Jason's face. Odessa states: "Sorry, son. You heard the announcement we've got to get you out of here." The husband of the couple responds: "Feel free to stay and pay your respects to Michael, we'll make sure he gets home."
Jason leaves with the couple in their car.
Many who fitted that age group hustle to vacate the streets immediately.

A SNITCH ON TIME

CHAPTER 6

The following evening a full curfew was put in place restricted to that Queens neighborhood, where Michael lived.

No one under 20 years of age was allowed to be on the streets after 9:00 PM or they would be arrested. These signs were posted on every telephone pole as well as inside and outside of grocery stores, business establishments and on the front windscreen of parked vehicles.

IT WAS NOW TUESDAY two days after Michael took that fatal bullet from the gun of NYPD Officer Eli Walsh.

Nothing was to be taken for granted by law enforcement in that small Queens suburban community.

It was clear. You step out of your house in that age category you'd better be back before nine in the evening.

The NYPD embarked on the neighborhood like it was a war zone at 9:00 PM with buses, vans, and armored vehicles. While, multiple NYPD helicopters circled aerially. Some dared and suffered the consequences as numerous arrests were made.

With most both young and old alike indoors, it seemed like the community was silently coming to grips with the gradual tugging away of their freedoms.

Michael held a job as a customer service representative at the local bank. Additionally, two part-time jobs at two separate accounting firms were no longer.

Outside the bank where he worked: Flowers and cards decorated the sidewalk as well as the bank's lobby. Many clients, saddened by the loss, while conducting transactions took some time to show their respect by chatting with other bank employees, still in mourning.

CHAPTER 7

While parents prepared their kids mentally and emotionally for the Saturday morning funeral only a few days away, the curfew remained in place. Gridlock traffic became a big problem for motorists as a major highway: The Cross Island Expressway runs through that rural Queens neighborhood.

A SNITCH ON TIME

Although many seemed to have kept their distance from the area, the buildup of vehicular traffic worsened.

Every street corner was sautéed with police activity 24/7. The eerie milieu felt as if civilians were being trained to run the streets of New York. At every turn, there was a cop, or an NYPD vehicle parked mobile, aerial or mounted. Using a military arsenal was part of their weaponry.

Meanwhile, at the police precinct, captains were busy drawing up enforcement plans for the funeral and thereafter. They feared the worse.

"Let's set up shop outside the cemetery. At least, they will be reminded that we are in control."

Said Captain Stiles to his colleague Captain Denny.

"If they were to try anything funny, the cemetery is right there."

Responds Denny.

So on Friday morning, the NYPD brought in reinforcement. They appeared ready to prowl in an instant. Despite the extended nightly curfew, tensions flared in the social media arena, mainly on twitter. Twitter tweets expressing dissatisfaction in the way the NYPD was handling the shooting tragedy.

For many, it was like salt in the wound of racial bias. Many who had been involved with bringing calm to the Borough of Brooklyn a few months prior when two cops shot and killed Kimani Gray, were still sore - so to speak.

"It is sad in this day and age that we as blacks are still humiliated and shot down because of the color of our skin."

Says Michael's dad to the pressing TV reporter.

"You were an activist in the shooting of the Brooklyn teen a few months ago. Clearly the 16 old was armed. How do you as a legal scholar feel learning that Michael was not armed but was shot as stated by the officer in self-defense?"

Asks the reporter.

"Michael did not even have a gun. You would be upset if a cop car collided with your brand-new car in a parking lot after failing to use his siren or emergency flashing lights. Cops know their job but so many fail to perform..."

"What do you think about the shoot first and ask questions later strategy. Do you think it should be outlawed?"

The reporter asks.

"It should. That's how they are able to shoot and kill our young people and then walk scot free."

Says Lawrence James.

"How is your 16-year-old son Jason coping with all this?"

Lawrence responds, "He is terrified, to say the least."

A SNITCH ON TIME

"I heard there is going to be a peaceful demonstration on Sunday. What do you think about this and are you going to be there?"
The reporter presses.
"It is a good idea, and I'll be there. However, the fact remains that an innocent teen is already dead. Who will be next?"
Responds Lawrence James.

LATER AT THE JAMES' FAMILY DISCUSSION, Jason complains about his dissatisfaction over the handling of the situation by the NYPD. "Once free to roam the streets in the neighborhood where I was born and raised, now I couldn't even go to the nearby Seven Eleven to buy a piece of gum."
Says Jason.
"When they brought in the rule to stop and frisk. Seventy-five percent of the kids they stopped and frisked were black kids, including Michael. You know that your brother never owned or wore pants that fitted below his butt. In Brownsville, Brooklyn in 2009, 93 out of every one hundred residents were stopped by NYPD, it was reported. Jason, they carry a gun, a badge, and the law. The breaking of this curfew could be a good excuse for another black teen to get shot by police."
Replies his Mom Odessa.

A SNITCH ON TIME

It is evident Jason was fighting this new lifestyle - losing his freedom.
On the other hand, throughout Floral Park, parents were reigning in their teens prior to the upcoming funeral on Saturday.

IT WAS NOW SATURDAY MORNING, and the funeral procession was filled with NYPD escorts, mourners, including Michael's peers, and many Government officials. Many tears were shed at the burial site.
Still the curfew remained intact for another night. The NYPD wasn't taking any chances in case rebellion was at the same time brewing in the minds of the youths in Queens and possibly other areas in New York.
On the following day Sunday, many churches devoted their entire service sessions to the healing of the community. It was evident that not only in Queens, but religious leaders in the entire New York area wanted to see something good come out of this. The healing process was emanating, at least in the minds of optimists.
Later in the evening, the peaceful demonstration began. People marched through the streets bearing signs. Others were still voicing their opinions on the shooting tragedy. Police officers joined in from behind their barricades paying attention to every detail.

A SNITCH ON TIME

The one block long event ended as members of the Clergy as well as activists addressed the audience of over 500. Gospel Artists in attendance entertained the assembly musically. Michael's parents Lawrence and Odessa James were also in attendance. They spoke about their loss and their commitment towards the healing process. At the close of their remarks, Odessa said:

"It's time to come together. Not only, to talk but to formulate some kind of strategy to deter some of the violence that're going on in our communities."

Many felt like it was water under the bridge or was it really?

A SNITCH ON TIME

CHAPTER 8

The trial was set to begin in a few weeks. Lawrence and Odessa James took it upon themselves to create and print flyers depicting defenseless young blacks who were gunned down by police. Each notice contained over one dozen unarmed blacks within the decade who lost their lives by a bullet discharged from the gun of a cop. Killings which police claimed were acts of self-defense.

A SNITCH ON TIME

With the jury of 12 already selected, the couple not only mass distributed these flyers but post them on every telephone pole in and around their neighborhood.

They even took it a little further and post them outside the courthouse. They did not miss a single telephone pole close to the courthouse. Odessa held the signs up while Lawrence drove the staples using a handheld staple gun. Where the staples did not penetrate they used back-to-back-adhesive tape to get the job done.

One night as they worked together two police officers in an NYPD cruiser surveying the area noticed these flyers on a Post No Bills backdrop.

The couple vanished as the cops pulled up leaving the stapling gun behind. The officers confiscate the object and with flashlights searched the area in pursuant to the two shadows. Lawrence and Odessa became oblivious by hiding inside a concrete culvert underneath the Boulevard.

Not seeing anyone the cops abandoned their search. Heading back to their cruiser, they got a close-up of their killings score. To them, this seemed like old news anyway.

THE HEARING IN THE CASE Michael James Vs NYPD Officer Eli Walsh was now moments away inside the Queens Courthouse. Even though there was no Michael James sitting inside the courtroom.

A SNITCH ON TIME

In New York, 2nd Degree Murder is codified under Penal Law 125.25. It is classified as an A-1 Felony and carries a maximum sentence of 25 years to life imprisonment. Eli Walsh could be sentenced for max if convicted in the shooting death of Michael James.

On the other hand, Walsh's partner in crime Officer Marcus Fenton was still hospitalized. It was reported that his medical condition worsened and was updated to a loss of consciousness.

Meanwhile, Lawrence James, not a practicing attorney but a member of the bar and authorized to work in New York State relinquished his pastoral duties and decided to defend his son in the case. You see, Michael stated in his will of trust that if the cause of his death was accident-related that he wanted his dad to represent him in court. His 19-year-old deceased son's wish was granted on time.

A SNITCH ON TIME

CHAPTER 9

Outside the courthouse, a huge demonstration involving over 300 teens was brewing. Placards and multiple signs are displayed. Kids chanting: WE WANT JUSTICE. WE WANT PEACE. WE WANT JUSTICE. WE WANT PEACE. HOLD YOUR FIRE MR. POLICE.

Defense lawyer Lawrence James stepped out of his car and was immediately swarmed by news reporters and cameramen. Using his briefcase, he warded off the pursuing crowd and pressed across the street and in front of the courthouse. As he ascends the granite steps back-dropped by the huge, tall granite pillars, he finds himself slowed by a TV Reporter who wouldn't let up.

"How do you feel about representing your son in the trial?"

"Great."

He answered pushing his way through.

"Is there anything else you would like to say?"

Asked the pushed aside reporter.

"I've got to get inside. Don't want to hold up the court's proceedings."

He finally gets past the entrance, breezed his way through security and enters the door to the interior.

Inside this not-to-modern courtroom, you can still breathe the smell of Pinewood from which the antique furniture emerged.

Lawrence James could not help reflecting on circumstances, which earlier delayed his arrival. Five minutes more and the clock on the wall in the rear of the courtroom would have its long hand on twelve and its shorthand on nine.

You see, prior to leaving his house, with Odessa already heading to the trial. He found himself having to convince their 16-year-old son Jason that he was not entitled to take that day off from school.

A SNITCH ON TIME

Lately, Jason has lagged behind. As a matter of fact, since the death of his brother Michael, he had missed the school bus and caught a cab to school on multiple occasions.

Anyway, Lawrence decided to shake this deterrent loose and focus on the trial at hand. Opening arguments were moments away.

A SNITCH ON TIME

CHAPTER 10

Odessa, emerged from the area of the ladies room and greets Lawrence with a go-get-them kiss. They meander to their seats. On his way, he stole a glance at Officer Eli Walsh dressed in an Italian designed black with gray pin stripe's suit. Next to him sits attorney Allan Flynn also neatly decked out.

A SNITCH ON TIME

The court announcer says:
"All rise," and introduces Judge Alexander McNeal. The Judge, a man in his 50s, white hair, and well-tanned strolls in wearing a robe that was made for him. His shirt collar says it was starched adequately, and his tie complimenting the wood furniture inside the courtroom.
McNeal sits down like a king on his throne between Old Glory and the New York State flag. Everyone is now seated. McNeal strikes the gavel as if conducting a test of the instructional tool.
The judge reminded the jury that this was a case in which a teen was shot and killed by a police officer and should be viewed only as such.
Mr. Allan Flynn scans the room.
"Mr. Flynn, your opening remarks,"
Says Judge McNeal.
Flynn stands and walks over in front of the Jury Box. He connects with Judge McNeal, who is writing on a white pad with a black pen. Flynn locks in with the jurors.
"Ladies and gentlemen of the jury: We are all aware that our police officers put their lives on the line daily in order to protect us. In any given incident, they never know what to expect. It is also a fact that black teen's commit crimes as well as teens of other ethnic groups.

A SNITCH ON TIME

Not only do these young people commit hideous crimes. They have the tendency to lie to a police officer when asked their age, and worst of all refusing to move when asked to do so.

In our society, 15% of teens expect to die young, according to the Minneapolis Star Tribune - June 29, 2009. The expectation linked to chancy behavior further states: Teenagers who engage in unsafe behavior may do so because they believe they're going to die young anyway, and may create a self-fulfilling prophecy with that belief. A study that tracked 20,000 kids in grades 7 through 12 found that 15% thought they would die before the age of 35. That group was seven times more likely to be diagnosed with AIDS. The fatalistic group was also more probable to do drugs, attempt suicide and get into fights that led to serious injuries. A pessimistic outlook was more common among Native American, black, and low-income teens, according to the study.

Teens in the United States make up almost half of all victims of violent crime over the age of 12. Teens from underserved populations, such as ethnic minorities and teens with disabilities, are often victimized at even higher rates than the general teen population. While most teens have limited access to qualified, age-appropriate victims services, teens from underserved populations have even fewer options. Often times, teens from underserved populations face additional challenges and barriers to accessing victim services. According to the National Crime Prevention Council (NCPC)

Max Wade, a 19-year-old Californian teen was recently convicted of a series of outrageous crimes included attempted murder and the stealing of a celebrity's Lamborghini.

It was said that the more police investigated him, the more shocked they became. At age, 16 Wade rappelled into a San Francisco dealership and stole $200,000.00 Convertible. Wade also planned to blow up Macys and had a helicopter ready to go.

Max Wade was eventually sentenced to life plus more than 21 years behind bars.

Seven black teens have been arrested on suspicion that they committed a hate crime when they attacked a 15-year-old Hispanic boy while he was walking home from school in Southern California, according to the Los Angeles County Sheriff's Department.

That March 14, 2014, beating in Palmdale was captured on video and posted on YouTube but has since been removed from the site. The seven boys, ages 13 to 16, were arrested for investigation of assault and committing a hate crime, Lt. Don Ford said.

A SNITCH ON TIME

The video shows as many as 10 boys surrounding the victim and challenging him to a fight. The suspects then began hitting the teen while others watched.
During the beating, the teens made racially derogatory statements that were captured on the video, Ford said.
After the victim fell to the ground, the assailants kicked him multiple times in the head, knocked out several teeth and left shoe impressions on his skin, Ford said.
The victim could get to his feet and escape the onslaught, and will need to undergo dental surgery.
The teens who were arrested were identified from the video, which was discovered by a Palmdale sheriff's deputy and has been retained for evidence.
At the time of this report, police were seeking three more suspects.
Officer Carlos King was working as a cab driver. On December 20, 1976, he picked up a teenage fare in Manhattan, drove him to Queens where the 15-year-old youth shot the officer to death and robbed him. King's shield was displayed indicating he had attempted to take police action. His revolver was still in its holster. The murderer was later arrested.
In this case Michael James Vs Officer Walsh, a crime which could have been prevented if it was not escalated.

A SNITCH ON TIME

Officer Walsh had to protect himself. By doing so, the life of a teen accidentally was lost. It could have been a kid of any race.

Allan Flynn strolls back to his side of the aisle.

A SNITCH ON TIME

CHAPTER 11

Lawrence James hears his name called. He approaches the lectern. He sees a reflection of himself, confirming that he's dressed the part. In the milieu of the courtroom, he sees 500 eyes looking at him. He gets rid of whatever butterflies remained in his stomach and masks the tears running down on the inside.

A SNITCH ON TIME

His assistant who arrived as soon as the courtroom doors opened had already loaded the projector slides for his opening. Lawrence James with some degree of authority faced the jury box, smiled, held onto the railing feeling and tapping on it gently as if touching the jurors' hearts one at a time. They felt the tug and reciprocated by zinging him.

"Nearly two times a week in the United States, a white police officer killed a black person during a seven-year period ending in 2012, according to the most recent accounts of justifiable homicide reported to the FBI.

This is a case in which a 19-year-old teen Michael James, who happened to be black, was shot and killed by NYPD Officer Eli Walsh on Sunday evening July 27, 2014.

The incident occurred after the officer driving a police cruiser at an erratic speed inside a 711 parking lot, without siren or emergency lights crashed into Michael James' BMW. When Michael James got out to investigate the damage and questioned the reasoning behind it, Officer Walsh opened fire and shot him in the chest. Michael James died a few hours later as a result of that gunshot wound to his heart.

This is not the first time a defenseless black youth has been shot and killed by a police officer.

In this decade alone over two dozen black youths were shot and killed by police. In most of these cases, the youngsters were unarmed."

A SNITCH ON TIME

The prosecution team confers among themselves as the light on the projector loads with the white screen diagonally in front of the room across from the jury box.

Timothy Stansbury Jr. picture is displayed on the screen:

"Unarmed and with no criminal record, 19-year-old Stansbury was shot and killed in 2004 in a Brooklyn, N.Y., stairwell. The officer who shot him said he was startled and fired by mistake. Police Commissioner Ray Kelly called his death "a tragic incident that compels us to take an in-depth look at our tactics and training, both for new and veteran officers." A grand jury deemed the shooting an accident."

Travares Mcgill: Picture is displayed on the screen:

Lawrence glances at his notes periodically as he continues his remarks.

"In 2005 in Sanford, Fla. (the same county in which Trayvon Martin was killed), the 16-year-old was killed by two security guards, one of whom testified that Travares was trying to hit him with his car. However, evidence showed the bullet that killed the teen hit him in the middle of the back and that the guard kept firing even after the car was no longer headed toward him."

Across the aisle, Allan Flynn on the defense team powers up his laptop computer.

Ronald Madison & James Brissette picture is displayed on the screen:

A SNITCH ON TIME

"In 2005, in the aftermath of Hurricane Katrina, five officers opened fire on an unarmed family on the east side of the Danziger Bridge, killing 17-year-old James Brissette and wounding four others. Next, officers shot at brothers Lance and Ronald Madison. Ronald, a 40-year-old man with severe mental disabilities, was running away when he was hit, and an officer stomped on and kicked him before he died. In a federal criminal trial, five officers involved in what have become known as the "Danziger Bridge Shootings" were convicted of various civil rights violations, but not murder."

Flynn readily engages in a web search on his laptop for verification purposes.

Sean Bell picture is displayed on the screen:

"In the early-morning hours of what was supposed to be 23-year-old Bell's wedding day, police fired more than 50 bullets at a car carrying him and his friends outside a Queens, N.Y., strip club in 2006. Bell was killed, and two of his friends were wounded. The city of New York agreed to pay more than $7 million to settle a federal lawsuit filed by the family and two friends of Bell. The three detectives who were charged, one of whom yelled "gun," although Bell was unarmed, were found not guilty of all charges. Recently, the NYPD fired four of the officers involved in the shooting for disobeying departmental guidelines on the scene."

Victor Steen picture is displayed on the screen:

"In 2009, 17-year-old Victor, who was riding his bicycle, refused to stop when chased by a police officer in a cruiser in Pensacola, Fla. In response, the officer aimed his Taser out of the driver's window and fired and then ran over the unarmed teen, killing him. This deadly incident was captured on video. A judge ruled that no crime was committed."

Oscar Grant: Picture is displayed on the screen:

"Oakland, California, transit police Officer Johannes Mehserle said that he accidentally used his gun instead of his Taser when he shot Grant on a train platform on New Year's Day 2009. The 22-year-old was lying face down with his hands behind his back, being subdued by another police officer when he was killed. Mehserle was convicted of involuntary manslaughter and sentenced to only two years for taking Grant's life. He was released after 11 months."

Ervin Jefferson: Picture is displayed on the screen:

"The 18-year-old was shot and killed by two security guards, also African American - outside his Atlanta home on Saturday, March 24, 2012. His mother says that Ervin was unarmed and trying to protect his sister from a crowd that was threatening her."

Kendrec McDade: Picture is displayed on the screen:

"Nineteen-year-old College student McDade was shot and killed in March 2012 when officers responded to a report of an armed robbery of a man in Pasadena, Calif. He was later found to be unarmed, with only a cellphone in his pocket. His death has prompted his family to file a lawsuit, in which

McDade's parents argue that he was left on the street for a prolonged period of time without receiving first aid. According to court documents, McDade's last words were, "Why did they shoot me?" The officers involved were initially placed on paid administrative leave but have since returned to duty.

Dane Scott Jr .: Picture is displayed on the screen:

"An Oklahoma jury convicted a 23-year veteran police captain of first-degree manslaughter in the death of an unarmed teenager who was running away after scuffling with the officer. Del City Police captains Randy Trent Harrison shot Dane Scott Jr in the back on March 14, 2012, following a high-speed chase that began when Harrison tried to pull over Scott's car."

Ramarley Graham: Picture is displayed on the screen:

"In 2012 Officer Richard Haste shot and killed 18-year-old Graham in the bathroom of his grandmother's Bronx, N.Y., home after a chase while he was attempting to flush a bag of marijuana down the toilet. Police did not have the warrant to enter the house, and Graham had no weapon. A grand jury charged the officer with manslaughter, but a judge tossed the indictment in May, ruling that the prosecution inadvertently misled jurors by telling them not to consider whether he was warned that Graham had a gun."

Trayvon Martin: Picture is displayed on the screen:

"Last year's killing of unarmed Florida's teenager Trayvon Martin by a neighborhood-watch captain who deemed him 'suspicious' and who claims that he shot the 17-year-old in self-defense sparked a heartbreaking national conversation about race and justice. His story is all the more tragic because it follows a familiar pattern. George Zimmerman's charged with second-degree murder walked away scot free."

Michael James: Picture is displayed on the screen: The same picture of Michael playing the piano at church.

"On Sunday afternoon, July 27th, 2014 Michael Emanuel James was shot and killed by NYPD officer Eli Walsh after his cruiser collided with Michael's BMW. Another unarmed black teen killing…

And the list goes on…There is nothing new for a black man without a weapon to be killed. It bears on the strategy: Shoot first, asks questions later. These unwarranted killings have to stop. It is my hope that our jurors will deliver the right verdict in this case."

Lawrence James takes his seat.

Judge McNeal eyes the clock on the wall and strikes the gavel. "This court is in recess until 9:00 AM tomorrow."

The court attendees file out. Much discussion sizzles among attendees as they exit.

CHAPTER 12

Outside the courthouse, the post-courtroom conversation lingers. A TV reporter presses as Lawrence James heads for his car.

"Mr. James, this ends the first day of what seems like it could be a long trial. How do you feel representing your son in this murder case?

A SNITCH ON TIME

"Michael is my son. I can't change that. However, I treat this case as I would have any other client. That is to give the best representation possible. Listen, I've got to get ready for tomorrow." Says Lawrence James.
"Mr. James it was nice talking with you. All the best to you in the trial."
Says the Reporter.
Odessa joins her husband as they board their automobile.
Attorney Allan Flynn heading in the opposite direction is aggressively pursued by another TV reporter.
"Mr. Flynn, your first day on the trial James Vs Walsh: It got really emotional in there hearing about all of these black teen shootings by police officers?"
"Like I said in opening statements: Our police officers put their lives on the line every day. Officer Walsh did."
"But the teen was said to be unarmed."
"When this case is decided, it will be the judge and jury not by Officer Walsh, the NYPD or myself."
"What do you think about the demonstration of over 300 people before the trial?'
"I am glad it was a peaceful one."

CONTINUED TESTIMONY opened with veteran detective Sam Black on the witness stands the next morning. He provided accounts of the crime scene with clarity to both the prosecution and defense.

Sam Black claimed that he arrived at the crime scene at 5:10 PM, ten minutes after Michael James was shot. He said that he checked Michael James for weapons, and he was unarmed, and according to paramedics who arrived at the same time still had a pulse.

The veteran detective also stated: the 2014 Porsche, owned and registered to Tacoma Stanley was facing south towards the Seven Eleven convenient store.

The 2014 BMW owned and registered to Michael James the deceased was facing east with a rolled down the front passenger window and about 3 feet from the passenger door of the Porsche.

The police cruiser driven by Officer Eli Walsh was facing north and apparently tried to squeeze its way between the Porsche and BMW at the time of the accident.

Furthermore, Michael James' body was discovered lying on the ground sideways with his head facing the northern area of the parking lot close to the adjacent street. Blood was gushing out of a bullet wound to the left section of his chest.

In regard to Officer Marcus Fenton who was in the passenger seat of the police cruiser, he said blood was oozing from a sustained concussion on his forehead.

A SNITCH ON TIME

The Officer's airbag malfunctioned. The detective's photo of the crime scene confirmed those details.

His partner, rookie officer Pete Malcolm concurred to those facts and added that Officer Eli Walsh was standing at the rear of the police cruiser when they arrived on the scene. His gun was also inside its holster.

At the end of Officer Malcolm's confirmation testimony, the court was recessed until the afternoon session.

A SNITCH ON TIME

CHAPTER 13

The afternoon session began. Over in the jury box, all 12 jurors looked refreshed and eager to get on with the proceedings. Judge McNeal wasted no time to bring the next witness, Abdullah Sadeik. He not only witnessed the shooting but is classified as a character witness.

A SNITCH ON TIME

"Mr. Flynn, your witness."
Says Judge McNeal.
Allan Flynn approaches the witness stand.
"Good afternoon Mr. Sadeik. Have you been paid or promised any form of payment for your testimony in this case?"
"No sir."
" And you swore to tell the whole truth."
"I did."
"Did you ever have or were planning on having a relationship, sexually or otherwise with Miss Tacoma Stanley one of the four people involved in the incident at the crime scene on July 27, 2014?"
"Objection!
Says Lawrence James.
"Objection sustained."
Says the Judge.
"Did you know Tacoma Stanley before that Sunday?"
"No. It was the first time I was seeing her."
"Did she leave you her business card upon checkout at the cash register?"
"She did not. I am happily married."
Says Abdullah.
"How many times per week you would say that Michael frequented your store or made a purchase?
" At least once or twice per week in my recollection"
Says Abdullah.

"Was he always by himself or accompanied?"
"It varied. Sometimes he was with a group who sounded as if they were rehearsing gospel songs."
"Thank you. No further questions."

CHAPTER 14

Its Lawrence James turn to questioning the witness.
"Sir your name is Abdullah Sadeik."
"Yes"
He replied.
"You were the MOD at the Seven Eleven in Floral Park, Queens on Sunday evening July 27 2014 when a black teen Michael James was shot.
"Yes, I was."
"How long have you been a manager at that location?"

"I've been the manager there for five years."
"Please tell the jurors and this court what you witnessed on that evening. When Michael James was gunned down by police."
"It was a busy evening as customers were flooding into the store after an all afternoon barbecues a few blocks away. Most of them picked up beer, wine coolers, and smoothies along with other snacks. A young lady had just left the store after purchasing a smoothie which most guys in the checkout line had volunteered to pay for. She ignored their act of chivalry.
Moments after her departure, I heard a crash. From my vantage point, I could see her standing outside the passenger door her black Porsche. A blue and white police cruiser collided with a BMW was next to that Porsche. I delegated the checkout assignment to my lone cashier to investigate what really went down. My first look was Michael standing behind the BMW. Then I heard a gunshot. I saw Michael fall to the ground, and the officer put his gun back in its holster. People were screaming, and the girl at the Porsche was yelling at the cop. The other officer in the cruiser looked like he was injured. I quickly called 911."
"You called 911?"
"What was the officer doing while you were on the phone?"

A SNITCH ON TIME

"He was arguing with the girl. I got scared thinking, he was going to shoot her next."

"Why did you think she could be next?"

"Objection! Yells Allan Flynn.

"Objection overruled. Answer the question," says, Judge McNeal.

"Because he threatened to arrest her for prostitution, and she dared him"

The Judge sits back, almost folding his arms while the jury takes copious notes.

"Was it the first time you were seeing the two officers, the girl and the gentleman who got shot?"

"Yes, except for the victim. He was a regular customer for more than three years. Most times he purchased a Raspberry Ice Tea and a pack of Tic Tacs."

"What was his demeanor like?"

"He was always jovial and at times either singing or humming a tune."

"Was he ever dressed in *Hoodies* or pants below his butt?"

"Objection! That's irrelevant!"

Says Allan Flynn.

"Objection overruled. You may answer the question" Says the Judge.

"He always dressed like he was going to be a special somebody."

A SNITCH ON TIME

"Thank you. Your honor, I have no further questions for the witness."

A SNITCH ON TIME

CHAPTER 15

The next two witnesses was Sister Bev, the church chorister and Natalie Graves the Branch Manager at the local bank where Michael worked.

Natalie a middle-aged Caucasian woman said that she was the one who hired Michael. In him, she saw a great potential. She recalled one day when a customer came

in and was frustrated about the pin assigned to her debit card not functioning. The client was very frustrated and wanted to terminate her bank account.
Although Michael was not the attending teller, he came out from behind his widow, engaged the customer after asking permission of the other teller. He assisted the customer who walked away smiling.
As a result, we not only retained her but received many referrals from her accounting firm. I was told that they later hired Michael on a part-time basis for their two New York locations.
Sister Bev, an African-American woman in her 50s stated that she persuaded Michael into joining the Church choir. His Dad had been trying to convince him into doing so for some time; she recalled. When Michael came on board not only did our music take on new heights, but our membership grew. People would come just to hear and watch him play the piano. There was a sweet spirit in the place.
In addition to the prosecution and the defense getting the scoop on Michael's character, the entire jury paid careful attention. Some took copious notes while others were caught in a thinking posture.
Next, on the witness stand was Dr. Preet Ellis, the physician who attended to Michael after he was brought to the hospital as a result of the bullet wound to his chest.

A SNITCH ON TIME

"My name is Preet Ellis."

"How long have you been a practicing physician?" asked attorney Lawrence James.

"I graduated from NYU School of medicine eight years ago. I've been practicing for the last seven years."

"Was Michael shot or stabbed?"

"Objection!"

Yelled Allan Flynn.

"Objection overruled."

Said the Judge.

"He was shot. I removed the bullet."

"From where was, this bullet removed?"

"We found it lodged directly behind his aorta in his backbone."

"Thank you, Dr. Ellis. No further questions your honor."

"My Flynn," summons Judge McNeal.

Allan Flynn approaches.

"Dr. Ellis, was this bullet you allegedly removed from Michael James' body kept as a souvenir?"

"All findings were handed over to the coroner's office."

"Who did Michael say shot him?"

"Objection your honor!"

Says Lawrence James.

"Objection sustained!"

A SNITCH ON TIME

Responded Judge Alexander McNeal.

"What did Michael James say, if anything while undergoing surgery to remove that bullet?"

Odessa James sitting next to her husband in the courtroom looks across at Flynn in amazement regarding his angle of questions directed towards Dr. Ellis.

"What is he getting at?"

Odessa asks Lawrence.

"He's just looking for loopholes in her testimony."

Responds Lawrence James.

"Nothing. I don't know how he survived for so long after that gunshot."

Says Dr. Ellis.

"No further questions."

Says Flynn after which he strolls back to his seat.

A SNITCH ON TIME

CHAPTER 16

It was the start of another day in the Michael James trial. So far, in this setting, it was clear that Allan Flynn was looking for any technicality he could find in the favor of his client.

On the other hand, Lawrence James already lost his son, Michael. He purposed in his mind that he wasn't going to lose this case. After all, it was the most important trial he has ever been associated with. Winning it for his son Michael was inevitable.

Inside the courtroom was seated witness Tacoma Stanley referred to as the *magnet*. Many in and outside the courtroom were anxiously waiting to hear her testimony. Meanwhile, the ballistics expert Robert Caldwell was on the witness stand.

"I've been working in ballistics for over 15 years." Says Caldwell.

"You were the one who opened the package in which the bullets' remains were transferred to your lab?" Asks Flynn.

"Yes, it was I, who opened the package."

"Was there any remnant from more than one bullet inside the package?"

"The remnants could only have come from one bullet."

"What type of bullet was it?"

"It was a 9mm NATO round."

"You also inspected the handgun retrieved from Officer Eli Walsh from the crime scene?'

"Yes, that gun was handed over to me by Officer Sam Black after the shooting incident."

"What were the specs on that gun, Mr. Caldwell?"

"It was an SIG P226, operated in a double-action mode only."

" After your examination of bullet and handgun would you say that the bullet was fired from that pistol?"

Asked Allan Flynn.
"Yes, it could not have been fired from any other weapon."
"Your honor, I have no further questions."
Lawrence James is called. He approaches Caldwell.
"Mr. Caldwell, was Michael James' fingerprint found on experiment #2, the gun which Officer Walsh used to shoot him?"
"No. The only prints found on the gun were those of Officer Walsh."
"Your honor I have no further questions."
Judge McNeal strikes the gavel. "The court is in recess for 15 minutes."
The court attendees file out.

IT WAS RUMORED that Tacoma Stanley was going to be called as the next witness in the hearing. Lawrence James took the time to go over documents in readiness for the star witness. She was one of four people who had witnessed the crime.
During this intermission Attorney, James' phone rang. It was the school principal at his son's Jason's school Mr. Stapleton. He reported that Jason had been involved in an altercation with another teen. The victim Brendan Charles alleged that Jason punched him several times in the stomach. The school police interceded and broke up the duel. As a result, Jason

was sent home suspended until further investigation. Several students came forward as witnesses.
"Is Jason okay? Do you need for me to come in and see you regarding this matter?" Asks Lawrence James.
"Not at the moment. Once we gather all the evidence we will meet with the parents." Says Mr. Stapleton.
"How are his parents? Was the press involved?"
"We spoke with his guardian. His parents are away on business and have been notified. They are on their way back for a meeting with our school's administration. Nothing is in the media as far as I know."
Says Mr. Stapleton.
"We will attend to this matter. Thanks for letting me know. Odessa and I thank you."
Mr. James hangs up and confers with his wife Odessa.

A SNITCH ON TIME

CHAPTER 17

Much unrest already colored this murder case. Today's hearings could create a serious dent into the suspected police cover up. "The court calls Tacoma Stanley," Says the Court Announcer. Tacoma steps up. After taking the oath, she readies herself on the witness stand. Allan Flynn was called on to cross-examine Tacoma.

A SNITCH ON TIME

Flynn busies himself and ambles towards the witness stand, engaging both the Judge and Jury before he lands there.

"Tacoma Stanley, you were one of the four witnesses at the scene when Michael Haynes, a black teen was allegedly shot by Officer Eli Walsh?"

"I was."

Says Tacoma.

"According to the report filed by Officer's Mason and Vasquez who questioned you at the crime scene, your home address was in Hicksville, Long Island. What were you doing in that Queens neighborhood?"

Asks Allan Flynn.

"I was invited to a block party and barbecue a few blocks away by one of my girlfriends who had moved there recently."

Says Tacoma.

"And what does your girlfriend do?"

"She's a registered nurse."

"Why weren't you at the so-called block party barbecue?"

"Objection!"

Says Lawrence James.

"Objection overruled."

Says Judge McNeal.

"I was delayed, being stuck in traffic on the Long Island Expressway."

A SNITCH ON TIME

"What time did you leave your house?"
"Objection!"
Says Lawrence James.
"Objection sustained."
Says McNeal.
"What time did you arrive in Floral Park, Queens?"
"It was almost 5:00 PM."
"Why were you at the Seven Eleven?"
"Objection. What is going on?"
Asks James.
"Counselor? Objection overruled."
"I had missed the event which apparently finished early. It was a hot day, and I went to the store to get a smoothie."
"Did you know the deceased Michael James before that evening when he was shot?"
"No."
"You've never met him before?"
Lawrence James is livid. His confusion with the direction of these senseless questions is visible on his face.
"Never had sexual relations with him over the phone or otherwise?"
"Never did."
"So why was he chasing after you in the parking lot before he crashed into Officer Walsh's cruiser?"

A SNITCH ON TIME

"He was just being friendly. The officer crashed into Michael's car trying to fill his quota."

"What do you mean his quota?"

"He was speeding after some other motorist. Maybe he needed one more citation for the month. You know how cops have to submit a certain amount of citations, legit or manufactured, especially if their total for that month is lagging. He was speeding without an activated siren or emergency flashing lights to catch his next victim."

Says Tacoma.

"Miss Stanley, I had no idea you worked for the police… what happened after the crash?"

"Michael got out and asked the cop what he was doing?"

"What exactly did he say to Officer Walsh?"

Eli Walsh is stone-faced as he listens to Tacoma's testimony.

"You Retard! You crashed my ride. What is the matter with you? The same thing I would have said in that situation. Then Walsh said something to his partner who was attempting to open the passenger door. Walsh stepped out of the cruiser and shot Michael James in the chest."

Says Tacoma.

At this point, she begins to cry.

A SNITCH ON TIME

"I have no further questions,"
Says Flynn.
He walks back to his seat.

A SNITCH ON TIME

CHAPTER 18

Levi James approaches. The witness touches her hair.

"Miss Stanley, you testified that it was your first time in that Queens neighborhood where Michael James was shot by NYPD Officer Eli Walsh.

"Yes."

"Did you have any trepidation?"

"No, I didn't. I felt like I was going to have a great time in Queens."
Says Tacoma.
"So were you at all disappointed?"
"Objection! That's speculative and leading."
Says Flynn.
"Objection overruled."
Says Judge McNeal.
"What chaos and police brutality!"
Replies Tacoma.
'Take the Jury back to what transpired immediately after the crash. You cited in your statement to police at the crime scene that Michael got out to view the damage and was upset."
"He was."
"Did he in any way threaten to shoot Officer Walsh or his partner Marcus Fenton?"
"Objection! Leading."
Says Flynn.
"Objection sustained."
Says the Judge.
"Did you see him pull any object like a gun, a knife or baseball bat on Officer Walsh?"
"No. He did not."
Replies Tacoma.
"What was Officer Walsh's demeanor when he stepped out of his car?'

A SNITCH ON TIME

"It was mean and cruel. After he shot Michael, it seemed as if he was going to shoot me next. He seemed - trigger happy."

Says Tacoma.

"Why would you say that?'

"I asked him why he shot Michael. He told me to shut up. Then he had to nerve to imply that I was a prostitute. His subtext said he would be very happy to erase me."

"Miss Stanley, you seem to be very detailed."

"That's what happened. I captured it all on video and immediately transferred it onto this flash drive."

"Your honor may I have your permission to show this video to the court."

Says James.

"Objection. Your honor, may I approach?"

Says Flynn, who is already on his way towards the Judge's table.

At the sidebar, Flynn argues about the authenticity of the video. "Your honor, what if the contents of this video have nothing at all to do with this case?"

James is persistent. "Your honor if this video details what happened at that crime scene, this can save the court valuable time."

"What if they are just nude pictures?"

Says Flynn.

A SNITCH ON TIME

"Let's meet in chambers. This court is in recess for 15 minutes."
says Judge McNeal.
They move to the Judges chamber. James takes his laptop with him.
"How long is the video?" asks the Judge.
"It looks like two and a half minutes long."
Says James.
"Too long, your honor. I feel we are taking away the juror's time from the case at hand."
Says Flynn.
"Let's watch the video counselors." Says Judge McNeal.
Lawrence James plays the video clip.
The clip depicts a great deal of hostility on the part of Officer Eli Walsh during his verbal confrontation with Tacoma Stanley at the crime scene.
"Counselors I rule to make this video an admissible piece of evidence. Let's return to the courtroom."
Says McNeal.
The trial reconvenes with most attendees anticipating a twist.
"I would like to inform the court that a new piece of evidence will be accepted into evidence as exhibit # 15. This is a video clip captured at the crime scene. Mr. James, feel free to play that video clip for the benefit of

the court before continuing hearing the witness' testimony."

Attorney James plays the clip.

Walsh shows his displeasure with Allan Flynn regarding playing of the video clip. Officer Walsh pays very little attention to clip.

The Jurors take notes as if it was Gospel.

Do you have any further questions for Miss Stanley?"

"No further questions."

"Mr. Flynn, do you have any rebuttal?"

"No, your honor."

"These court recesses until tomorrow afternoon at 1:00 PM.

The courtroom clears out.

OUTSIDE THE COURTHOUSE reporters gather in droves. They surround Eli and Odessa James.

"Mr. James, we are hearing reports that your 16-year-old son Jason was involved in an altercation at school and has been possibly suspended. How are you and your family dealing with this? And do you think you'll be able to continue the trial?"

Asks the TV reporter.

We were notified but have no idea what started this. As soon as we are thoroughly informed we'll be able to make an assessment. As far as the trial is concerned, we are here to stay."

A SNITCH ON TIME

Says Lawrence James.
The couple departs hastily.

A SNITCH ON TIME

CHAPTER 19

For Lawrence and Odessa James, the clock to the rear of the courtroom was ticking away, and now their hearts were pounding faster due to their 16-year-old son's dilemma at school. They were due back in court the following day, and a new challenge presented itself – Jason's suspension.

A SNITCH ON TIME

It seemed like it was divine intervention for Judge McNeal to schedule an early afternoon continuation of the trial for the following day. He didn't say why. Maybe it was for personal reasons. Anyway, Lawrence and Odessa were prepared to take advantage of this so-called favor.

As the couple drove home together, Odessa asking herself but addressing Lawrence at the same time: "What is wrong with Jason? Couldn't he see that we are in the midst of a trial, and we don't need any mud thrown at us?"

Lawrence listened for a moment longer after Odessa finished her multiple question summation.

"We don't know all the details of what went on at his school. However, it seems like underneath the surface Jason is reacting to the death of his brother. They've been together for over 16 years. He always looked up to Michael. This could be very tough on him. I'm not saying that should give him the right to initiate a fight if that's what he did, but it can have a side effect."

Odessa was getting ready to respond as they immediately pulled up in front of their driveway and into a nest of cameramen and reporters.

Before both doors of the car opened, microphones from multiple TV channels were waiting to be stuck in their faces.

Lawrence is pinned by one reporter who asks:

A SNITCH ON TIME

"Mr. James, you seem to be doing well at the trial resulting from the death of your son, Michael. However, it seems like family life is falling apart, with the recent suspension of your son, Jason. Do you see yourself withdrawing from the rest of the hearings? What are your plans at the moment?"

On the other side of the car, Odessa is swarmed by multiple TV reporters as well.

"There is no reason to withdraw from the trial at this point. First, we will need to find out what really went down at the school."

Says Lawrence James.

"But they are saying that your son punched the other kid first in his stomach,"

Says the reporter.

"Our plans are to meet with the school administration and the kids parents ASAP."

The reporter on the other side finally gets his chance at Odessa James.

"Mrs. James, it has been said by members of your peers that you have great family values. Do you see yourself being able to support the rest of the trial with all this coming to you?"

"Michael wanted his Dad to represent him, and that's what we are doing. Everything else which looks like a smokescreen will eventually dissipate. We've got business to take care of."

A SNITCH ON TIME

Says Odessa James.

With Lawrence James leading the way, Odessa frees herself from the mob of cameramen and reporters. The couple enters their house flustered.

A SNITCH ON TIME

CHAPTER 20

Inside the house on the living room's couch, Lawrence and Odessa find Jason, scared and discombobulated as he watches the news about his suspension repeat itself. Lawrence accesses the remote and turns off the TV. Both parents engage Jason in conversation.

They learned from Jason that the other kid Brendan involved in the altercation had been taunting Jason

ever since his brother got shot. Jason told them that he was at the point of avoiding school because of the numerous taunting incidences. According to Jason, Brendan attacked him first saying: "You black kids give our police trouble. That's why your brother got popped. Its drug's money he used to buy that car. Then he pushed me, and that's when I punched him"
"Did anyone witness this Jason?" asks his dad.
"Several kids did. I don't know if they might be too chicken to come forward."
"Get your homework done and get some rest," Says his mom.
"We'll be driving you to school tomorrow."
Says his dad.

THE COUPLE SEEMED burdened with multiple things on their minds. Lawrence saunters to their office next to the living room. Odessa heads to the kitchen.
Lawrence James accesses his computer and browses to an NYPD site. His search results is ACCESS DENIED. He tries again, still access is denied.
Odessa walks in with two cups of coffee. She notices Lawrence's backside and him looking out the window. He seems occupied looking at the traffic lights and the late-night traffic. Odessa puts one cup of coffee on the desk next to the computer. The movement deactivates the screen saver. On the screen, it reads ACCESS

DENIED. She walks over to Lawrence and hands him the other cup of coffee.
'So how is it going?"
She asks.
"Looking at the traffic,"
Lawrence responds.
" Access denied?"
Asks Odessa.
"Yep. This whole trial is taking a toll on me, complicated by Jason's behavior."
"We can't walk away from it, Lawrence. Michael is our son. He wanted you to represent him."
"Our family life is being tossed like an open book into the public arena."
"You are a public figure, what else would you expect?"
"This has gotten to be too much."
After stroking his head and shoulders, Odessa looks over at the computer and moves towards it. She tries accessing the failed NYPD site. ACCESS DENIED is the only information she sees. Staring at the screen, she yells.
"Bastards! You are concealing information from the public."

A SNITCH ON TIME

CHAPTER 21

Looking at her husband still staring out the window, Odessa asks. "What do we know about these guys?"

"They are a powerful fortune 500 company. They would do just about anything to rake in revenue while minimizing their expenditures."

Says Lawrence.

A SNITCH ON TIME

"Last year it was reported: NYPD officers wrote over $400M in citations."

Lawrence is still looking out the window. Odessa sips on her coffee.

"Rumor has it: Some of their captains get paid under the table for keeping a lid on the amount of overtime they allow to officers."

Says Odessa.

"Their 34,500 plus officers serve a population of 8.2 million people. That's not enough cops per civilian for all the money they bring in."

Says Lawrence as he finally moves from the window and sits on the couch behind Odessa.

Lawrence continues: "It's no wonder that most of their officers who have shot and killed black teens walk away unscathed. There were only a few cases they lost and were made to pay millions in lawsuits."

"The New York Civil Leadership Union sued them to get data on the stop-and-frisk program as well as the race of people shot by officers. That is still to be settled."

Odessa continues: "New York Times sued the NYPD in 2010 seeking records on pistol permits, bias incident data, the department's crime incident database and its Freedom of Information Law logs. The NYPD has a habit of not complying with FOIl no matter what's the request.

A SNITCH ON TIME

Lawrence's head is bopping as he is now sunk into the comfortable couch.

Odessa pays no attention to her falling, asleep husband. Instead, she continues: That same year an NYPD officer faced retaliation from the department after blowing the whistle on extensive efforts by his supervisors to juke the stats."

"What else do we have?" Asks Lawrence, waking up.

"Wait a while, Lawrence, we've got a friend in Google.

Odessa inputs Google's URL.

"There is more on them.

Dirty Little Secrets in NYPD's Internal Affairs Bureau."

"Let's print that." Says Lawrence.

"There is something here about them denying a request for records in the shooting death of the 16-year-old black teen Kimani Gray. The kid was shot seven times - four in the front and three in the back. That killing was carried out execution style."

"I attended that funeral. It was tough on his parents. Print that also."

Says Lawrence.

Lawrence continues: "Is there anything about them paying off a hospital to keep one of their officers in a coma for an extended period of time, in order to withhold his testimony in a murder case?"

Odessa searches but comes up empty.

"There's nothing."

She says.
Lawrence snores in the background.
"You are sleeping, honey. I've got this."
She goes to the bedroom and returns with a comforter.
She throws it over Lawrence and kisses him on the lips.
Lawrence wraps himself up in the warmth of the bed cover.

A SNITCH ON TIME

CHAPTER 22

Odessa moves to the living room and dials a number on her cell phone. Delores Knight, the nurse who had invited Tacoma Stanley to the block party on the night when Michael was shot, answers.

"Delores, what time do you get off from work?" Asks Odessa.

A SNITCH ON TIME

"I'm already off, OJ."
Replies Delores.
"Could I borrow one of your uniforms?"
Asks Odessa.
"I have nothing clean at the moment. I do my laundry tomorrow afternoon."
Says Delores.
"Put one in the wash. I'll pick it up in two hours."
Says Odessa.
"Since when you became an undercover?"
Asks Delores.
"Girl a woman must do what she must support her man."
Responds Odessa.
Odessa puts herself together to look like Delores Knight. Staring in the mirror she says: "I remember Michael saying: 'Most black women do look alike;' maybe because our ancestors originated in Africa."

LATER, Odessa knocks on Delores' door. Delores opens surprised. "Well, I'll be darned. Come on in twin sister."
Delores give Odessa the uniform on a hanger along with a hat and ID badge in a bag. "You are on your own, OJ."
Says Delores.
Odessa exits speedily.

A SNITCH ON TIME

Later, Odessa arrives at the hospital adorned in nurse's attire. She snoops around, bypassing NYPD security. She surveys the floor where Officer Fenton rooms. An NYPD Officer gait.
It's now early morning and time is against Odessa. Finally, she sees a nurse coming down the hallway pushing a cart. Her name badge reads Rosemarie Solomon.
"You are traveling too slow Rose. What room did we send you to?"
"Room 112: that police officer who's unconscious."
Odessa grabs the cart. "I've got this, poor guy. They need you to change bed sheets in 256 for the incoming patient. Pick up the cart when you're finished.
Odessa wheels the cart past additional police security and into room 112.

A SNITCH ON TIME

CHAPTER 23

Odessa finds Officer Fenton still unconscious except for gentle rolling of the eyes. After checking officer Fenton's blood pressure and temperature, she plants a magnetic recording device underneath the bed attached to the metal bed frame. She changes the bed sheets and exits.

A SNITCH ON TIME

BACK AT THE HOUSE a few hours prior, Jason woke up after a restless night and knocked on his parent's bedroom door. There was no answer. He called out:
"Mom, Dad! Are you guys in there?"
Still there's no answer. So he pushes the door. The room is vacant. 'Dad, Mom where are you guys?"
He does not get a response.
Jason looks inside the living room. His parents aren't there either. He saunters to the office. On the couch, he finds his Dad still fast asleep. Next to him is a handwritten note signed by his mom. It reads: Lawrence, you needed your sleep. So I didn't bother to wake you. I am out getting information for the trial.
Jason under his breath says:
"Since when you became a Private Investigator, Mom? What is going on in this house? Dad, wake up. Is Mom okay?"
Lawrence breathes in the morning air. He gets up looks at Jason and strolls to close the open window through which he viewed the traffic many hours ago.
"Did your Mom finish printing those confidential documents on the NYPD?"
Asks Lawrence.
"The printer tray is not only full but additional pages are all over the floor. Here's the note she left you."
Says Jason.

A SNITCH ON TIME

Pass me my phone. Why are you having a heart attack? I'm sure your Mom is okay. She can handle herself."
Says Lawrence.
Jason is still flustered.
Lawrence dials her number and gets her voicemail.
Jason walks out of the room.
"Jason we've got to get to your school at 9:30, in less than an hour, so get ready.
Lawrence gathers the documents from the printer and places them inside a folder. He then goes through all rooms in the house to satisfy his curiosity.
Lawrence readies himself, first he visits the bathroom. Inside the bedroom, his cell phone rings. He misses that call. Lawrence is now dressed for a busy day and heads to the car with Jason behind him.
Lawrence realizes that he does not have his cell phone and returns to getting it. He's now heading out towards the car and gets ready to redial. Odessa's car pulls into the driveway. Odessa steps out.
"I wish you would give more detailed information regarding your whereabouts. What's up with that new look?"
Says Lawrence.
"We've got a big day ahead of us. I've accomplished much in the last few hours. Should I dress now for the trial or would I have time to change after the visit to Jason's school?"

A SNITCH ON TIME

Says Odessa.
"You look great. Let's play it by air."
"Mom since when you look like Delores Knight?"
"Your Mom could be embarking on a new career. Let's go pay principal Stapleton a visit."
Odessa steps in on the front passenger seat and immediately begins rearranging her makeup.
'So anything I need to know, undercover lover?"
Asks Lawrence as he drives away the yard.
"Just put your phone on voice to text mode. Even so, also select the save to voice option in case you need to replay the audio later."
"Thanks for the warm blanket."
"You are welcome."

A SNITCH ON TIME

CHAPTER 24

The James' family pulls up at Floral Park High, Jason's school. They head towards the principal's office. A student sitting on a bench in the schoolyard reading from a Math book yells out.
"Jason you are back! Yeah!"
"Who is that?"
asks his mom.

A SNITCH ON TIME

"Felix Santos, he's from my Math class. He wants to become a Mathematician some day."
Replies Jason.
"Did he witness the fight between you and Brendan?"
Asks his Dad.
'No, but his girl Denise was there. She was leaving the cafeteria when Brendan came up to me initiating a fight."
Says Jason.
"Hold on a minute. Let's call Felix over here."
Says his Dad.
"Felix! Do you have a minute? My parents want to meet you."
Hey, but I don't want to get involved. I didn't see anything."
Says Felix.
"That's okay Felix. We are not putting you under any pressure. I am Lawrence, and this is my wife Odessa.
Says Lawrence.
"I know. I see you guys on TV at the courthouse every day on the evening news."
Says Felix.
"Yes. We've got to get back there soon. We are trying to bring calm to this situation. We need your help."
Says Lawrence James.
"I wasn't there but my girl Denise saw what happened. She videotaped it on her iPhone. She told me she was

going to put it on Youtube, but I told her I didn't think that would be a great idea."
Says Felix.
"Where is Denise now?"
Asks Odessa.
"She's in class,"
Says Felix, who's now smiling from earlobe to earlobe.
Looking at Jason, he says: "I'll see if I can get Denise to meet your Public Figures Parents.
Jason smiles underneath.
'Tell her we are waiting to meet her."
Says Odessa.
Moments later, Felix returns with Denise holding on tightly to her iPhone.
The couple introduced themselves and asked Denise if she would be willing to accompany them to settle the pending situation with Brendan's parents, the school principal, the assistant principal and guidance counselor.
Denise agrees and follows them.
"We got your back!"
yells Jason as Felix's returns to the schoolyard bench and the reading of his Math book.

A SNITCH ON TIME

CHAPTER 25

They arrive at principal Stapleton's office. Brendan and his parents are already seated inside. Brendan's face turns red with a look of apprehension when Denise walks in behind Jason's parents. Lawrence and Odessa introduce themselves to White couple. The Guidance Counselor a Caucasian man in his 40s walks in followed by Assistant Principal Miss Stevens, who commands a Jamaican dialect.

Lawrence James apologized for taking up Principal Stapleton's time but thanked him for giving them the opportunity to come in and see him.

"I know you are inundated with goings-on at the trial, and now this. Why don't we get to the root of the matter and find out what really went down? I must preface by saying: If Brendan was wrong, our strict school policies will require he be punished. And if Jason was wrong as I have been told the equivalent applies. I must let all parents associated know that it is too fragile a situation to have both in the same class in our school at the moment. Denise, are you one of the students who witnessed the altercation?"

"Yes."

Responds Denise.

Mr. Welch, the Guidance Counselor chimes in. "Jason has been falling behind in his studies since the shooting incident involving his brother. Not only, that his attitude has gone south."

"Mr. Welch, while we thank you for the observation. That's not what we are here for. If a cop had shot your brother or a sibling who you look up to, I am sure you would be affected to a certain extent.

Says Jason's mom.

A SNITCH ON TIME

"We don't need for this to get further out of hand. It is already all over the news."

Says the Assistant Principal as she holds up the Newspaper, headlined: Son of Attorney Lawrence James Will Serve Suspension for Fighting in School.

"Let's just get to the bottom of this."

Says Brendan's dad Mr. Charles.

"We are not here to defend our son. If he's wrong, he deserves to be punished. A video was captured detailing the incident."

Says Lawrence James.

"Let's watch the video says Mr. Stapleton.

Denise hands her iPhone with video clip already cued to her principal. He presses play, and they watch the video clip.

The clip shows Jason leaving the school cafeteria. Brendan runs out after him and proceeds to taunt him. Brendan says: "I am glad your brother got shot. He tried to become a cop killer. Styling off in his drug mobile."

"Jason says: "Stay out of my face Brendan."

Several students follow them yelling: Fight! Fight! Fight!

Jason punches Brendan several times in his stomach. Brendan falls to the ground, and School Police steps in. The video ends.

"My apologies Mr. and Mrs. James; a different version of the story was relayed to me."

Says Mr. Stapleton.

"We had no idea this is what occurred, or we would not have taken the story to the Newspaper."

Says Brendan's Mom.

Why didn't you present this video after the incident, Denise?"

Says the Guidance Counselor.

"I didn't want anyone to shoot me or my *homies*." Says Denise.

Brendan's parents are livid.

"We as an administration do not tolerate fights or racial comments at Floral Park High. Our faculty is made up of just about every race on the planet. Jason, we are not going to lift your suspension. You still could have walked away from the fight. We will reduce it by one week. You will instead serve a one-week suspension. Nevertheless, you must make up your classes."

Says Stapleton.

Brendan's parents stare at each other feeling their son is going to get the max.

"Brendan, you were engaged in a double whammy. Plus sources told me this morning you had been taunting Jason for days prior. You will serve a three-week suspension. Plus you will have to find time to make up your classes.

Jason's parents and Brendan's parents shake hands. Jason walks over to Brendan, shakes his hand and says: "I'm your brother even though I am Black, and you are White."

Brendan's parents are teary eyed.

Jason and his parents thanked Denise and the administration. They leave the office.

The local TV channel scheduled an interview with Brendan's parents regarding the fighting incident for later that evening. That interview was subsequently canceled.

A SNITCH ON TIME

CHAPTER 26

Levi and Odessa James are on their way to the courthouse and the reconvening of the trial. Odessa, having had time to change her wardrobe looks very upbeat. Lawrence, on the other hand, is extremely focused. With Jason's situation at school now behind them, they turn their full attention to the trial. In their minds, this could be the day Officer Eli Walsh begins his testimony.

A SNITCH ON TIME

Back at the hospital, two NYPD captains pay Officer Marcus Fenton a timely visit. The captain duo of Stiles and Denny walks in dressed in their NYPD uniforms. They observe Fenton while assessing his condition.
"I think the rest is doing him good."
Says Stiles to Captain Denny.
"He shouldn't be in any rush to get out of here. By the time, he regains consciousness this whole trial should be behind us."
Says Denny.
Fenton rumbles and stretches trying to pull himself up out of the bed. The NYPD captains are alarmed. Even though it has been almost six weeks since he fell in a coma.
They radio the police station. "Dead Man Moving." Captain Howard at the station receives the transmission. He answers back. "I didn't copy."
"Fenton is moving!"
says Stiles.
"Make sure he doesn't rush that recovery process." says Howard returning to his office."
"We'll be back to check on you tomorrow."
Says Stiles.
They depart the hospital.
Inside Lawrence and Odessa's car and on their cell phone, they read the text and entertain an audio playback.

A SNITCH ON TIME

"Great job Odessa. Where did you learn this stuff?"
"We've been married for 25 years. I think I am still entitled to some mystery."
Responds Odessa.
They park the car and are approaching the vicinity of the courthouse.
Cameramen, as well as reporters, pursue the couple.
"By now, now they must have received the news regarding Jason's revised suspension,"
Odessa says under her breath.
Suddenly multiple microphones are stuck in their faces.
"Mr. and Mrs. James, Now that you have brought calm to the situation involving your 16-year-old son Jason and that misreported altercation incident, do you have anything to say to the public?"
"We believe in Justice. We believe in Peace. Therefore, Justice and Peace will take its course."
Says Odessa.
The couple makes their way inside the courtroom.

CHAPTER 27

The atmosphere inside the courtroom is tense. It seems like more attendees are crammed into the courtroom on this particular day. Looking across the room several uniformed NYPD officers are seated.

Lawrence James, along with his wife Odessa arrives and stares in wonderment at the additional police presence. "Was Officer Eli Walsh back on active duty?" They reasoned looking into each other's eyes as they took their seats.

The court announcer says:

"The court calls Eli Walsh." Lips mumbled as Officer Walsh, sharply dressed approached the witness stand. He swore to tell the truth and took his seat.

"Your witness Mr. James,"

Says Judge McNeal, cleaning moisture from his Ray Ban pair of chic glasses.

Lawrence James walks up to the lectern, peripherally connects with the jurors and releases the second button on his Giorgio Armani gray with the light gray pinstriped jacket.

"Good Afternoon, Mr. Walsh."

He says.

"Good Afternoon."

Responds Eli Walsh.

"Are you conscious of that oath you just took?"

"Yes, I am."

"And that is to tell the truth and nothing but the truth?"

"That is the oath I just made."

"Thank you, Mr. Walsh."

"Your name is Eli Walsh, that's correct?"

"It is."

A SNITCH ON TIME

"Eli Walsh, how long have you worked with the NYPD?"
"Fifteen years."
"Fifteen satisfied years?"
"Objection!"
Yells Allan Flynn.
"Objection sustained."
Says Judge McNeal.
"The NYPD is a great institution to work for, isn't that so?"
"Objection!" Yells Flynn once again.
"Objection sustained. Counselor, where is this heading?"
"Your honor I want to make sure that officer Walsh was employed by the NYPD at the time when he shot Michael James, and that he understands the motto of that institution which is Courtesy, Professionalism, Respect: CPR."
"I understand the acronym and what it means."
Responds Officer Walsh.
"You won't do anything to tarnish those standards, would you?"
Asks Lawrence James.
"What do you mean?"
"Officer, you understand tarnish: smear, smudge, blemish, taint, and discolor?"
"Why should I?"

"I don't think you would. After all, they trained you and paid you to do the job which they employed you to perform. So you won't discolor, taint, blemish, smudge, smear or tarnish the NYPD."

"No."

"What were you doing in the parking lot on the evening of July 27th, 2014, prior to shooting and eventually killing the 19-year-old black teen, Michael James?"

"I was on the lookout for traffic violators."

"Inside the parking lot or on the street?

"Objection."

Says Flynn.

"Objection overruled. Answer the questioning officer."

Says McNeal.

"I was on the lookout for traffic violators on the street."

"Were you engaged in a speed trap, using a radar gun, etc."

"I was mainly looking out for motorists who ran the red light or made illegal turns at that intersection."

"How long were you there prior to the accident involving Michael James' BMW?"

"A few minutes."

Answers Walsh.

"Did you catch or cite anyone?"

Asks Attorney James.

"Objection! That's official police business." Says Flynn.

A SNITCH ON TIME

"Objection sustained."
Says the Judge.
"Who was your accompanying officer?"
"Officer Fenton, Marcus Fenton."
"Was he senior to you, junior or a rookie?"
"He was Junior."
"How much Junior, would you say?"
"He's been on the force for at least five years."
"Was that the first time you and Officer Fenton had been working together in a patrol car?"
"We've teamed up on multiple occasions."
"What type of a cop was he, jovial, comedic, hard-nosed?"
"It really depends on... All of the above at varying times."
"Do you consider him a racist?"
"Objection! Speculative."
"Objection sustained. Be careful counselor, you are border lining."
Says Judge McNeal.
"Was he hard-nosed when it came to blacks or was he jovial or comedic?"
"Your honor, may I approach."
Says Allan Flynn.
"You may."
Responds Judge McNeal.

"You honor. I think this is a waste of the juror's time, listening to all of these leading questions."
Says Flynn.
"Your honor, Officer Fenton, Walsh's partner who was inside the patrol car at the time may never be able to testify in this case. I believe it is fair the jury knew the mindset of those two officers before the accident, which sparked the shooting death of Michael James that Sunday afternoon."
"Mr. Flynn you would have your chance."
Says McNeal.
The two lawyers return to their positions.
"Mr. Walsh, you are not a racist, are you?"
Objection!
Says Flynn.
"Objection sustained."
Says the Judge.
"Officer Walsh, you love all races of people. Would you say?"
"I do."
Says Walsh.
"Why did you leave the parking lot in such a hurry and neglected to activate a siren or emergency flashing lights of the NYPD cruiser of which you controlled."
"I was chasing after a motorist. Apparently, those devices malfunctioned."
"Apparently?" asked Lawrence James.

Walsh responds.
"Yes, apparently."
"Did you check those devices before driving away from the station?"
"We did."
"Did you check them after they failed to function when crashed into the BMW?"
"I didn't,'
"Why not?"
"I had no time."
Lawrence James goes to his desk at the defense section and retrieves some documents. He returns and faces Officer Walsh on the witness stand.
"Officer Walsh, this is an inspection log supplied by an independent Motor Vehicle Inspection facility which carried out a thorough inspection of the unit you were driving at the time of the accident. It says that all emergency devices were functioning. The left head lights and left indicator bulbs were damaged along with bumper and left fender as a result of the crash."
"Objection. We don't have a copy of that log."
"I'm surprised you don't."
Says Lawrence James.
"Counselor, will you be sure to have copies of that inspection log for tomorrow's setting. This court is adjourned until tomorrow morning at 9:00 AM."
Says McNeal.

A SNITCH ON TIME

The court attendees file out.

A SNITCH ON TIME

CHAPTER 28

Outside the courthouse, multiple cameramen as well as reporters aggressively surround Attorney Allan Flynn. "Mr. Flynn, your client Officer Walsh during his testimony said that he was not a racist. What were his motives for shooting a black teenager who was unarmed?"

Flynn seemed to be avoiding the question.

"Do you care to comment?"

Asks the reporter pressingly.
"Walsh is entitled to defend himself in that incident. It could have been someone from another race who got shot instead."
Says Flynn.
"According to Attorney James, the inspection logs indicated that the patrol car's emergency lights and siren were functioning prior to the crash. Why did Officer Walsh neglect to activate those devices?"
"I believe that my client has and continues to state the facts in this case."
Says Flynn.
"How is his partner doing in the hospital?"
Asks the reporter.
"I heard he is recuperating. That's a good sign."
Says Flynn as he strolls towards the parking lot.

ON THE FOLLOWING MORNING, Captain Stiles and Denny visit Officer Marcus Fenton at the hospital. To their surprise, Fenton was not only sitting up but drawing with crayons on a piece of paper. The illustration shows the early stages of the crime scene prior to the accident. Additionally, there is an arrow directly where the crash occurred. In front of the arrow, Fenton writes the sum of $500,000.00.
They try deciphering the sketch.

A SNITCH ON TIME

"What is he trying to say? This looks like the crime scene but the money?"
Asks Stiles.
"Fenton, you've got to help us out buddy."
Says Denny.
Fenton remains mute.
"So Fenton, how are you feeling? Are you going to talk to us soon? At least, you can draw us pictures. This is a major improvement since our last visit. We've got to get back to the precinct. We just wanted to check in on you. Hang in there."
Says Denny.
"We'll try to figure out that half a million dollars." Says Stiles.
"Could he be referring to that reward money on Raymond Benedict?"
Denny asks.
"I can't believe Benedict has been on the loose for so long and none of this so-called crime busters has been able to bring him in. They claim we don't give them overtime hours, but they fail to cash in with the 40 hours they have."
Says Stiles.
"That's a chance for them to pick up some extra money. Yet they complain. Just bring in Benedict. Our Chief would be happy."
Says Denny.

A SNITCH ON TIME

The two NYPD captains notice that Fenton has fallen asleep. Officer Stiles confiscates the illustration. Stiles and Denny leave the hospital and are driving back to the precinct.

Officer Denny makes a phone call. Eli Walsh picks up on the other end. "Walsh, this is captain Denny, I'm here with Stiles. That was a great job you did in court yesterday. We realize that you are no longer on the team at the moment, which could only be a temporary situation..."

"Thanks but no thanks gentlemen. None of you guys stood up for me, so I could keep my job. I've got a mortgage to pay while dealing with this trial."

Responds Walsh.

"Why don't you go after Benedict? That money is still on the table. It doesn't matter if a civilian rope him up," continues Captain Denny.

"I appreciate the call gentlemen, but I've got to head back to court. Let's talk about this at another time. Shall we?"

"We've got your back, Walsh."

Stiles voices over.

A SNITCH ON TIME

CHAPTER 29

Inside Judge McNeal's courtroom, the trial continues with Officer Eli Walsh on the witness stand. McNeal before calling Lawrence James ruled that the inspection logs for the police patrol car involved in the accident be added to the evidence in the case as exhibit # 16.

"Mr. James you may continue."

Says McNeal.

A SNITCH ON TIME

Lawrence James approaches the lectern in continuation of his cross-examination of Officer Eli Walsh.

"Good morning Officer Walsh."

"Good Morning."

"Officer, I am a little troubled that you did not use the siren as well as the emergency lights, which were both functioning in that patrol car used by you to pursue a most-wanted criminal."

"Objection. Your honor, we do not have any reference to the motorist who was allegedly being pursued. Nor do we have a witness who verified such."

Says Flynn.

"Objection sustained."

Says McNeal.

"Officer Walsh, this log in my hand verifies that you did not use emergency equipment installed in your patrol car while pursuing a suspect. However, let's move on."

Walsh does not respond.

Lawrence James makes eye contact with the jurors before continuing.

Meanwhile, conversation brews among Allan Flynn's team.

"Officer Walsh before crashing into Michael James' BMW on that fatal evening, did you notice a black

Porsche parked on the right of that driveway in the mall?"
"Yes. I did."
"You did? Officer, did you notice the Black BMW coming from the other side of that driveway?"
"I did not."
"Did you notice the African-American woman, Tacoma Stanley standing outside of that black Porsche on the other side?"
"I did."
"Did you think she was hot?"
"Objection!"
Says Flynn.
"Sustained."
Says the Judge.
"On a scale of 1-10, how much did she appeal to you sexually?"
"Objection."
"Objection sustained."
"Did she look like the type of woman you would have gone to bed with?"
"Objection. Leading."
"Objection sustained. Counselor?"
Says McNeal.
"Officer Walsh, why did you call Miss Tacoma Stanley a prostitute?"
"Because she walked and talked like a prostitute."

"What physical evidence did you have? Did you sleep with her? Did any of your buddies sleep with her?"

"No. However, I know a prostitute when I see one."

"If you were so sold on the fact that she was a PROSTITUTE, why didn't you arrest her for attempting to pick up a client?"

"That would have been my next move."

"And you didn't. But instead, you shot and killed a defenseless 19-year-old black teenager after colliding with his BMW? Why did you shoot Michael James, knowing that he was unarmed?"

"Because he was coming at me as if he wanted to shoot me."

"Did he point a weapon at you? Did he say he was going to shoot you? Did Tacoma Stanley, who you claimed was a prostitute say 'shoot him?' Did he push his hands inside his pocket attempting to pull out a weapon?"

"No, but he looked like he had intentions. So I had to defend myself."

"Is that what you were taught at the police academy?"

"No. Nevertheless, after years on the force, I have seen and understand survival tactics, which were not taught to me back then."

"Like shooting to kill?"

"No. Shooting in self-defense."

A SNITCH ON TIME

The Judge looks at the clock on the wall at the rear of the courtroom.

"This court is now in recess for one hour."
Says McNeal as he strikes the gavel.

A SNITCH ON TIME

CHAPTER 30

Odessa meets with Tacoma Stanley at Starbucks. They choose the high chairs versus the lows. They sit down for a quick coffee.
"How are you doing, Tacoma?"
Asks Odessa.
"I'm doing great. I just can't wait for this trial to end, and Walsh gets thrown in the slammer."
She responds.

A SNITCH ON TIME

Odessa reaches inside her briefcase and pulls out a manila folder. From the folder, she retrieves an 8x10 portrait of Raymond Benedict. "Have you ever seen this guy?"

Asks Odessa.

"I thought you were going to ask me something in regard to your son's death."

Says Tacoma as she returns the picture.

"It is regarding his death."

Responds Odessa.

"How come? I was there when the cop shot Michael and even recorded the video."

Says Tacoma.

"We know all that. Please take a good look at the picture."

Tacoma takes another look and ponders over it.

"I think I saw him at the Seven Eleven. He was there with two other guys. He was wearing a baseball cap. They were standing in front of me in the checkout line. They were even trying to pay for my smoothie. I told them: No Thanks."

"Where did they go after that?"

"They went outside. When I walked out the store they were getting in their car."

"What Make and Model was the car?'

"It was a Ford Mustang. A brown one."

"Did they drive away immediately?"

"I know they were drinking Heineken. Not sure when they left."

"Did you see them there after the accident?"

"No. They weren't there."

"When you got out of the store, did you see the NYPD patrol car in the parking lot?"

"To be honest, I did not notice until they crashed into your son's car."

Odessa's phone beeps. She checks it.

"Excuse me."

Says Odessa.

She places a call.

Her husband Lawrence picks up.

"Lawrence, check your phone. You have multiple text messages. See you soon honey."

"Tacoma, are you prepared to give this testimony in court if called upon?"

"Anything to help, Mrs. James."

"Thanks. We are due back in the courtroom in 15 minutes."

Odessa departs hurriedly.

WHILE ODESSA JAMES MET with Tacoma Stanley at Starbucks. Captain Stiles and Denny once again visited Officer Marcus Fenton at the hospital. To their surprise, Fenton was sitting up, very responsive and talking except with a stutter.

A SNITCH ON TIME

"You are making swift progress."
Says captain Stiles.
"You don't want to rush it, Fenton. Your job is there when you are ready."
Says captain Denny.
"I know…but I feel…I am missing something." Says Fenton as he utters his first words since the crash almost six weeks ago.
"You aren't missing a beat."
Says Stiles.
Captain Stiles phone rings. He answers it. Walsh is on the other end driving to the courthouse.
"Hey Stiles, I've been considering what you and Denny told me. I can go after Benedict if you guys provide me with a cruiser and a pistol. Someone told me where he hangs out."
"Walsh, that is a little too much to ask. Why don't you go after him with your own vehicle? We don't want to get caught up in this. Make it a civilian's arrest. Alternatively, tell us where he is. We'll go get him and split the half a million with you."
"What if the judge gives me the max. How do I collect from you guys?"
"It was a self-defense issue. Those types of cases always get thrown out."
Says Stiles.

A SNITCH ON TIME

"Hey Walsh, FYI, your partner is up and about." Says Denny.
"Tell him not to rush his recovery. I am doing great. I've got this."
Says Walsh.
"Put him on the phone," Continues Walsh.
They give Fenton the phone. He almost drops it. After its retrieval, he says: "Hey Marcus…I am doing…well. Talk with you …soon."
The nurse walks in with a cart. On it noticeably, is a meal of assorted fruits. The captains make their exit.

A SNITCH ON TIME

CHAPTER 31

Odessa meets briefly with Lawrence inside the courtroom moments before the trial continues. Lawrence quickly checks all of his text messages. Moments later, testimonies continue with Officer Eli Walsh on the witness stand. Allan Flynn steps up from across the aisle.

A SNITCH ON TIME

"Officer Walsh, was it your intention to shoot and kill Michael James?"
Asks Allan Flynn.
"No. It wasn't. I felt the lives of my partner Marcus Fenton and myself were threatened. I responded and as a result, he got shot."
"Have you ever seen or met Michael James before the shooting incident?"
"Yes."
Odessa and Lawrence are somewhat surprised.
Walsh continues.
"I had stopped and frisked him a few months earlier in Jamaica, Queens."
"Was he armed when you frisked him?"
"No. He wasn't."
"What was his demeanor? Did he say anything that was in any way derogatory to you?"
"He said I should spend my time dealing with real crime. He also said I should get my hands off him."
"What prompted you to stop and frisk him?"
"He was leading a boisterous group and getting in the way of traffic."
"Did you hear what they were saying?"
"No, but it was very visible."
Odessa looks at Lawrence and says: "They were singing. He told me about it. However, he never said it was Walsh."

"So in your mind, they were disruptive, him and his posse?"
Asks Flynn.
"Yes."
"Take us back to what happened on that Sunday evening when the same teenager you stopped and frisked a few months ago got shot."
"Our patrol car was parked at the Seven Eleven on Hillside Avenue and Little Neck Parkway. We saw a motorist make a right turn from the left-hand lane at that intersection. We attempted to pursue the motorist. Michael James drove across in front our cruiser in his BMW. With no place to go, we crashed into him."
Says Walsh.
"Did Michael James in any way try to obstruct you from carrying out that chase?"
"I would think so. Yes."
"What happened after that?"
"He jumped out from the driver's side and angrily proceeded towards me."
"Did you have your gun out of the holster at this point?"
"Yes. I had to protect Officer Fenton and myself. He continued pursuing me, and that's when I shot him."
Officer Walsh, did you plan on shooting Michael James to kill him?"

"No. I did not. He was enraged as if he was going to do something terrible to me. I had to defend myself."

"No further questions." Says Flynn and then takes his seat.

"Mr. Walsh, you may step down. The court might find it necessary to recall you at some point. This trial reconvenes on Monday at 1:00 PM."

Says Judge McNeal.

CHAPTER 32

It's Sunday evening, one day shy of six weeks since Michael James was shot by the bullet from NYPD officer Eli Walsh's gun.

Many mourners assemble at the Seven Eleven parking lot to sing, pray and light candles. They felt the need for solidarity. Not sure this would impact the outcome of the trial.

A SNITCH ON TIME

Attorney Allan Flynn seemed as if he was tactfully trying to have his client walk scot free as has been done in so many of these shot in self - defense cases. Odessa James was providing her husband Lawrence with some very important undercover NYPD police information by tapping into Fenton's hospital room. Even so, that information may not be admissible in court. The judge could easily throw all of that out and call it witness tampering.

Anyway, the crowd at the prayer vigil was growing. Someone replaced the dried-up flowers with fresh ones. The backdrop with the portrait of Michael playing the piano, now sunburnt and saturated with water stains was removed by Brendan and Jason. Brendan's parents assisted Jason's parents with the lighting of fresh new candles.

The church choir showed up and immediately began singing some of Michael's favorite songs. Moments later, Tacoma Stanley and Nurse Delores showed their faces for a few minutes.

More and more attendees from that block party, which Michael attended before he was gunned down showed up and joined in the singing.

Other kids from Jason's school attended. Felix and Denise strolled up holding hands.

Michael's ex-boss from the bank and some of his co-workers were also in attendance.

Michael's parents Lawrence and Odessa James addressed the gathering. Odessa pleaded for unity in the community and applauded Brendan's parents for being there and showing their support. Odessa reminded the mourners that the trial was still not over, but she believed that justice will be served. Lawrence James said he looked forward to not just a better and more unified Floral Park community but the whole of New York City.

A SNITCH ON TIME

CHAPTER 33

The Monday Afternoon session of the trial began inside the packed Judge McNeal's courtroom. Inside the jury box, the jurors seemed relaxed after an extended weekend break. Over that weekend, the news broke: Michael Brown, an 18-year-old black teen was gunned down by police in Ferguson, Missouri. Police said that the teen was unarmed.

A SNITCH ON TIME

Many teens took to the streets, looting as well as demonstrating, chanting: "We Want Justice. We Want Peace. Police sprayed them with tear gas in order to maintain peace.

On the other hand, Police would not release the name of the cop who shot Brown. Lawyers representing Brown's family blasted the decision, suggesting authorities were protecting one of their own rather than following standard procedures. Releasing the name of the officer who shot and killed the teen in Ferguson, Missouri, isn't as important, said a high-ranking police officer, as protecting the community and the person who pulled the trigger. President Obama even addressed his gripes about the way in which the police was handling the situation.

The FBI launched an investigation in this shooting. Brown was getting ready to head off to college the next day. His mother called him her gentle Giant. His Dad called him a leader and a problem solver. Like Michael James, he also had a younger brother who adored him.

THERE EXISTED A SENSE OF EAGERNESS to get on with the trial. Judge McNeal seemed enthusiastic as when he was announced to the court a few weeks ago. Old Glory and flag of the Empire State gave the impression they were raised a little higher and apparently laundered over the weekend.

A SNITCH ON TIME

The Judge announced that there was new evidence in the case, and the court would like to spend the time exploring such.

The court called Tacoma Stanley, and we were on our way for yet another day of hearings in the Michael James Vs Officer Eli Walsh murder trial. Miss Stanley was a returning witness to the surprise of many in the courtroom.

Judge McNeal called Allan Flynn's name, and he rose to the occasion. He shows a portrait of Raymond Benedict to the witness.

"Miss Stanley, did you see the gentleman in that picture, Raymond Benedict, follow you into that Seven Eleven?"

Asks Flynn.

"No. I did not."

"Did you see him in the checkout line?"

"Yes. I did."

"Do you know if he was following you?"

"No. Why should he?"

"Did Mr. Benedict ask for your business card?"

"No, he did not."

Says Tacoma.

"No further questions."

Says Allan Flynn as he takes his seat.

Next, the court calls Attorney Lawrence James. On his face, he showed signs of nearing the finish line. His

wife and valuable aid, in this case, smiles as he stepped forward.
Miss Stanley was flaunting a new hair style.
"Miss Stanley, during your testimony a few days ago, you mentioned that it was your first time in the Floral Park, Queens neighborhood, where Michael James was shot and killed. Yes?"
"Yes. It was my first time."
Says Tacoma.
"You testified: It was very much a wake-up call for you?"
"It was."
"Take us back to what happened immediately before the accident while you were inside that Seven Eleven. You stated that you were in the checkout line, and it was very long. Do you recall who was a front of you in the checkout line?
"Yes. There were three guys. They wanted to pay for my smoothie."
Lawrence James retrieves an 8x10 portrait from a folder.
"You testified earlier that you have seen this person before?"
"Yes. He was one of the guys in the checkout line."
"Was this the first time you saw Mr. Benedict?"
"As much as I could recall. Yes."

"What did you say to him when he offered to pay for your drink?"
"I told them no thanks."
"Did you see him again after they left the Seven Eleven?"
"Yes. They got inside a Ford Mustang with a bottle of Heineken each in their hands."
"You videotaped the confrontation with you and Officer Walsh. This is now part of the evidence in this case. Did you see Raymond Benedict and his posse during or after your verbal exchange with Officer Walsh?"
"No. I didn't."
"Were you aware that the person in this picture, Raymond Benedict was most wanted by the NYPD and there was a $500,000.00 reward for his capture?"
"I had no idea."
"Thank you, Miss Stanley. I have no further questions."

A SNITCH ON TIME

CHAPTER 34

Officer Walsh received very little support from captain Stiles and Denny. It was clear to Walsh that if he wasn't going to disclose to them Raymond Benedict's whereabouts, the two police captains weren't going to assist him in bringing in Benedict.

Plus, Walsh was suspended without pay and was financially unable to pay them upfront for rendering any of those favoritisms: such as the acquiring transportation, a pistol, and necessary backup.

INSIDE THE COURTROOM, Judge McNeal recalled Walsh to the hot seat.
"Mr. Flynn. Your witness."
Says McNeal.
Feeling the venom of James' questioning of Tacoma Stanley, Allan Flynn straightens his tie, re-buttons his jacket and saunters towards the witness.
"Officer Walsh you shot Michael James in self-defense?" Is that right?"
"Yes. I had no choice he was coming at me. So I shot him in self-defense."
"Thank you. Your honor, I have no further questions."
Says McNeal.
Lawrence James' name was called, and he approached as if he was getting ready to put Officer Walsh in a vice and tighten it gradually.
"Officer Walsh, it is my understanding that Raymond Benedict was a most-wanted man by the NYPD. He was on the run for more than one year.
They wanted him off the streets because since he became at large more and more people stayed off the streets. Benedict was involved in a series of drive-by

shootings in Staten Island leaving ten people dead. The reward for information leading to his capture was $500,000.00. Every cop in the NYPD wanted to cash in, including you."

"Objection!"

yells Allan Flynn.

"Objection sustained."

Says McNeal.

"That reward money was appealing to you Officer Eli Walsh?"

"There's nothing wrong with turning someone in for a reward. After all, he was wanted."

"So, in your desperation to collect that sum of money:

- You raced through a crowded parking lot.
- Neglected to activate your patrol's car emergency devices.
- Collided with another motorist who you afterward shot and killed.
- Lied to the court and said that you were chasing after a motorist who made an illegal turn when you knew that you were chasing after Raymond Benedict, a most wanted by the NYPD.
- It is my opinion that you have not only committed murder by killing Michael James, but you have perjured yourself by lying to this court multiple times during this trial."

"My testimony is correct."

Says Walsh.
"Officer Walsh, were you wearing a body camera during the shooting incident?"
"No. I wasn't."
"May I ask why not?"
"I wasn't wearing one."
"I don't see why you didn't wear a body camera when they were made available. It shows police transparency; unless you had something to hide.
No further questions."
Says James as he returns to his seat.
"The court calls Officer Marcus Fenton.
Says the court announcer,
All heads are turned followed by murmurings. Walsh is weak-kneed heading back to his seat. Judge McNeal strikes the gavel.
"Silence in court! Be seated. I want to remind you that this is my courtroom and not a concert hall. Please keep your applause to yourself."
Says the Judge as he brings the boisterous courtroom to order.

A SNITCH ON TIME

CHAPTER 35

Officer Marcus Fenton who appeared from the back of the courtroom is now on the witness stand. Cameramen and reporters try pressing their way inside the courtroom. Fenton takes the oath. The court calls Allan Flynn's name. All eyes, they are on him as he approaches the witness.

A SNITCH ON TIME

"Officer Fenton, you've been in a coma for almost six weeks. Is that true?"

Asks Allan Flynn.

"That's what they told me." Answers Fenton.

"How do you remember so much to bear an accurate testimony?"

"I can see it all unfolding like it was yesterday."

"Your honor, is it okay if we take a break so our witness could recuperate?"

"Do you need a break Officer Fenton?"

"I'm doing great. Your honor."

"Please continue counselor."

"Officer Fenton, I know the NYPD is not paying you for this testimony. As a matter of fact, you are still employed by them. Who is picking up the tab?"

"No one."

"You are not paid by any institution or any Church organization?"

"Objection.

Says Lawrence James.

"Objection sustained."

"I noticed your physician is in the courtroom. Is that for precautionary measures?"

"He cleared me for this testimony. I had no idea he was here."

"Two years ago your assignments were reduced to desk duty for misrepresenting the facts in a dispute with captain Stiles. Yes."
"Objection, your honor."
Says James.
"Objection sustained."
"Have you ever been convicted of a felony or crime involving moral turpitude?"
"I haven't."
"You know what it is to lie. And … to do so in front of your peers, the jury, and this entire courtroom: You know that the act of doing so is perjury. A crime punishable by up to 3 to 7 years in prison, a fine of up to $5,000 or both?"
"I know what perjury is. It hurts when black teens are shot and killed, and my law enforcement peers walk away and get rehired to possibly do the same thing. I could not lie there in that hospital bed and allow this to happen."
The courtroom is once again noisy.
The Judge strikes the gavel.
"Silence… Mr. Flynn did you have a further question for the witness?"
"No further questions."

A SNITCH ON TIME

CHAPTER 36

The court calls Attorney Lawrence James.

"Officer Marcus Fenton, first I must applaud you on your remarkable recovery."

Says Lawrence James.

"Thank you."

Responds Fenton.

A SNITCH ON TIME

"How are you feeling?"

"I feel great."

The jurors leaned forward, sitting on the edges of their seats.

Lawrence James goes straight for the jugular by presenting the 8x10 portrait to Officer Fenton.

"Officer, have you seen this picture before today?"

"Yes. That is a sketch of Raymond Benedict, most wanted by our department."

"And how much was the reward for information leading to his capture?"

"$500,000.00."

"Half a million dollars! Were you excited about collecting that sum of money?"

Asks James.

"I don't think there was anyone on the force who wasn't, including police captains. Every cop on the NYPD wanted to catch Benedict. Some even voiced ignoring the issuing of parking tickets, so they can be on the alert, in case he drove by."

"Did you see him at the mall on the evening when Michael James was gunned down by your partner, Officer Walsh?"

"He was there."

Murmurs continue in the courtroom.

Allan Flynn wants to object, but he is confused as to what he should object to.

A SNITCH ON TIME

"Where was he?"

"Objection."

Says Flynn.

"Objection overruled."

Says McNeal.

"Where was Raymond Benedict?"

Asks Lawrence James.

"He took off in a Ford Mustang, brown in color."

Says Fenton.

"Did your partner Officer Walsh, who was driving the patrol car in which you occupied the passenger seat attempted to pursue Benedict?"

"Yes. We did."

"And what happened?"

"He crashed into the black BMW."

"And what happened after the crash?"

"The driver of the BMW, Michael James came out to check the damage. He was upset and said 'Retard. You crashed my ride. What's the matter with you?'

"Do you recall the exact words used by your partner when he crashed into Michael James' BMW?"

"Objection! Hearsay."

Says Flynn.

"Objection overruled. Answer the question."

Says Judge McNeal.

A SNITCH ON TIME

"He said: Darn, we missed Benedict. That Nigger is trying to get laid got in the way. Why doesn't he pay attention to what's coming through?"

Most of the jurors are caught taking copious notes. Meanwhile, the defense team shows signs of uneasiness.

"What did Officer Walsh do as Michael James got out of his patrol car?"

"He said: You called me a retard. I'll show you who's retarded. And shot the kid. When asked why he did that? He said the black kid got in his way."

"Did Michael put his hands in his pocket or threatened to shoot Officer Walsh?"

"No. He looked like he was just assessing the damage done to his car. He was upset."

"Did Officer Walsh use offensive or derogatory remarks to Tacoma Stanley, who witnessed the incident?"

"Objection."

"Objection sustained."

Says the Judge.

"What did your partner say to Tacoma Stanley?"

"He told her to shut up, or he could have her arrested for prostitution."

Lawrence James mops his brow.

"No further questions."

He says and returns to his seat.

A SNITCH ON TIME

You could hear a pin drop inside the courtroom.
"This court is in recess. "
Says Judge McNeal.

CHAPTER 37

Closing arguments began after the brief break. Allan Flynn steps up, and this time, more than ever he engages the entire courtroom.

"Ladies and gentlemen of the jury, the NYPD is a great organization. Every day its officers put their lives on the line to protect you and me. They should be applauded.

I don't believe that its officers go out on patrol looking for potential young black men to shoot and to kill. These hard-working men and women in uniform lives are at risk 24/7 because of what they do. They get very little respect from those who they work hard to protect. I trust that you will make the right decision when you present your verdict. I don't think my client Officer Eli Walsh intended to shoot Michael James, but he had to defend himself."

There's complete silence.

Allan Flynn returns to his seat next to Officer Walsh.

Lawrence James as customary stepped up and immediately engages the 12 jurors.

"Almost two months ago Michael James was shot and later died of a gunshot wound to his heart. The defendant in this case Officer Eli Walsh pulled the trigger. Michael was unarmed.

Over the last decade, police officers have been responsible for the shooting deaths of over one dozen unarmed African-American youths. In an effort to walk away from those crimes scot free, those officers claimed it was either an accident or those young victims were shot in self-defense.

In a sword defense duel: one fighter comes against the other with a sword drawn. Simultaneously, in a gun defense, two weapons should be engaged. There is nothing for a cop to defend if a weapon is not drawn on them in that duel situation.

In police tactics, self-defense has become overrated. It is a combination of two words used by cops when their intention was to kill an unarmed black kid and walk away unpunished for that crime. Cops are of the mindset to shoot and kill instead of controlling the civilian.

They are intentionally killing off our future black leaders. They can no longer stop and frisk here in New York, so now they continue to shoot and kill. In this case, the agency involved is the NYPD.

Clearly, this outfit will do whatever it can in order to limit expenditure while concealing information in regard to incidents such as this. Shoot first and ask questions later, is a cop out. Shooting someone in self-defense is a cop out when no weapon is drawn by that civilian. Michael James was shot and killed moments after racial slurs were used towards him by Officer Walsh. These types of killings have to stop. Officer Eli Walsh should be punished for this crime. "

Odessa James, smiles as Lawrence walks back to his seat.

"The jury will deliberate and return a verdict in three days."

Say Judge McNeal.

The court attendees file out.

A SNITCH ON TIME

CHAPTER 38

After three days of jury deliberating, New Yorkers were anxiously awaiting the verdict in this case. If found guilty of second-degree murder in the shooting death of Michael James. Officer Walsh could be sentenced up to 25 years to life.

On the other hand, it was customary that the majority of cops who shot black teens, claiming it was a self-defense - walked away unpunished.

A SNITCH ON TIME

The crowd outside the courthouse was gradually growing in numbers as well as in decibels. Several cameramen as well as reporters gathered in droves. Some were occupied in the setting up of equipment.

Demonstrators assemble with signs and placards reading: NO PEACE, NO JUSTICE. ANOTHER UNARMED BLACK TEEN SHOT AND KILLED.

Police survey barricades in anticipation of the worst.

The news media at the site was still busily unraveling the latest news about the 18-year-old black teen, who got shot recently by police in Ferguson, Missouri.

By this time, they had just released the name of the Officer who shot Brown, Darren Wilson a 28-year-old White veteran police. They also released footage prematurely of Brown involved in a strong-arm robbery prior to being shot by Wilson.

INSIDE THE COURTROOM, a buzz of uncertainty lingered. Lawrence and Odessa James strolls inside the courtroom and headed straight to their seats.

On the other side of the room, Officer Walsh looked at times as if he was sitting on needles. Flynn standing next to him no doubt acted as support to calm his nerves.

Judge McNeal was announced. He walked in focused as ever. All rose and then quickly took their seats.

A SNITCH ON TIME

McNeal made contact with the jurors sensing their readiness.

"Is the verdict ready?"

Asks McNeal.

"Yes, your honor."

says the jurors.

"May Officer Walsh, please stand."

Says Judge McNeal.

Walsh stands up.

"May the Foreperson, please stand and read the verdict."

Says Judge McNeal.

"On count one of perjury? The jury finds the defendant Eli Walsh guilty."

Says the Foreperson.

There is an "ah" inside the courtroom.

"Silence please!"

Says McNeal striking the gavel.

The Foreperson continues.

"On count two of second-degree murder? The Jury finds the defendant Eli Walsh guilty."

"The jury has spoken. Sentencing will be set one week from today."

Says Judge McNeal.

The courtroom erupts on the prosecution's side of the aisle.

A SNITCH ON TIME

CHAPTER 39

THE SENTENCING

Unrest continued, accentuated by days of curfew in the shooting death of Michael Brown in Ferguson, Missouri. A similar case: in which a White police Officer shot and killed a black unarmed teen.

An overnight curfew has been imposed and the National Guard, the U.S. state militia, has been deployed in the St. Louis suburb of 21,000 people to stop looting and burning that have punctuated the protests.

It was claimed: The disturbances are the worst of their kind for more than a year. In July 2014, angry teen clashed with police after Michael James was gunned down by police in Queens, New York. The NYPD Officer Eli Walsh was found guilty of perjury and 2nd-degree murder.

In July 2013, there were angry, albeit peaceful, protests in cities across the United States over the acquittal in a Florida second-degree murder and manslaughter trial of neighborhood watch volunteer George Zimmerman, a white Hispanic, who shot dead and killed a defenseless black teenager, Trayvon Martin, in the street during a scuffle in February 2012.

President Barack Obama and civil rights leaders appealed for calm while a federal investigation into the shooting proceeds.

"While I understand the passions and the anger that arise over the death of Michael Brown, giving into that anger by looting or carrying guns, and even attacking the police, only serves to raise tensions and stir chaos," Obama told a news conference.

"It undermines, rather than advancing, justice."

A SNITCH ON TIME

MEANWHILE, INSIDE THE QUEENS COURTHOUSE, sentencing in the Michael James Vs NYPD Officer Eli Walsh case was handed down.
Judge Alexander McNeal sentenced NYPD Officer Eli Walsh to 5 years in prison plus a $5,000 fine for perjury in the case in which he shot Michael James, the 19-year-old black teen from Floral Park, Queens. Plus, 20 years to life for 2nd Degree Murder in the same case.
Walsh was sentenced to a total of 25 years to life in prison without parole. Many thought it was a harsh sentence. On the other hand, others felt it was time for the justice system to reprimanded horrific policing.

About The Author

A SNITCH ON TIME

John A. Andrews hails from the beautiful Islands of St. Vincent and the Grenadines and resides in Hollywood, California. He is best known for his gritty and twisted writing style in his National Bestselling novel - Rude Buay ... The Unstoppable. He is in (2012) releasing this chronicle in the

French edition, and poised to release its sequel Rude Buay ... The Untouchable in March 2012.

Andrews moved from New York to Hollywood in 1996, to pursue his acting career. With early success, he excelled as a commercial actor. Then tragedy struck - a divorce, with Andrews, granted joint custody of his three sons, Jonathan, Jefferri, and Jamison, all under the age of five. That dream of becoming all he could be in the entertainment industry now took on nightmarish qualities.

In 2002, after avoiding bankruptcy and a twisted relationship at his modeling agency, he fell in love with a 1970s classic film, which he wanted to remake. Subsequent to locating the studio which held those rights, his request was denied. As a result, Andrews decided that he was going to write his own. Not knowing how to write and failing constantly at it, he inevitably recorded his first bestseller, Rude Buay ... The Unstoppable in 2010: a drug prevention chronicle, sending a strong message to teens and adults alike

Andrews is also a visionary, and a prolific author who has etched over two dozen titles including: Dare to Make a Difference - Success 101 for Teens, The 5 Steps To Changing Your Life, Spread Some Love - Relationships 101, Quotes Unlimited, How I Wrote 8 Books in One Year, The FIVE "Ps" for Teens, Total Commitment - The Mindset of Champions, and Whose Woman Was She? - A True Hollywood Story.

In 2007, Mr. Andrews a struggling actor and author etched his first book The 5 Steps to Changing Your Life. That title having much to do with changing one's thoughts, words, actions, character and changing the world. A book which he claims shaped his life as an author with now over two dozen published titles.

Andrews followed up his debut title with Spread Some Love - Relationships 101 in 2008, a title which he later turned into a one-hour docudrama.

Additionally, during that year, Andrews wrote eight titles, including Total Commitment - The Mindset of Champions, Dare to Make A Difference - Success 101 for Teens, Spread Some Love - Relationships 101 (Workbook) and Quotes Unlimited.

After those publications in 2009, Andrews recorded his hit novel Rude Buay ... The Unstoppable as well as Whose Woman Was She? and When the Dust Settles - I am Still Standing: his True Hollywood Story, now also being turned into a film.

A SNITCH ON TIME

New titles in the Personal Development genre include Quotes Unlimited Vol. II, The FIVE "Ps" For Teens, Dare to Make A Difference - Success 101 and Dare to Make A Difference - Success 101 - The Teacher's Guide.

His new translated titles include Chico Rudo ... El Imparable, Cuya Mujer Fue Ella? and Rude Buay ... The Unstoppable in Chinese.

Back in 2009, while writing the introduction of his debut book for teens: Dare To Make A Difference - Success 101 for Teens, Andrews visited the local bookstore. He discovered only 5 books in the Personal Development genre for teens while noticing hundreds of the same genre in the adult section. Sensing there was a lack of personal growth resources, focusing on youth 13-21, he published his teen book and soon thereafter founded Teen Success.

This organization is empowerment based, designed to empower Teens in maximizing their full potential to be successful and contributing citizens in the world.
Andrews referred to as the man with "the golden voice" is a sought after speaker on "Success" targeting young adults. He recently addressed teens in New York, Los Angeles, Hawaii and was the guest speaker at the 2011 Dr. Martin Luther King Jr. birthday celebrations in Eugene, Oregon.

A SNITCH ON TIME

John Andrews grew up in a home of educators; all five of his sisters taught school - two acquiring the status of school principals. Though self-educated, he understands the benefits of a great education and being all he can be. Two of his teenage sons are also writers. John spends most of his time writing, publishing books and traveling the country going on book tours.

Additionally, John Andrews is a screenwriter and producer and is in (2014) turning his bestselling novel into a film.

See more in: HOW I RAISED MYSELF FROM FAILURE TO SUCCESS IN HOLLYWOOD.

Visit: www.JohnAAndrews.com

Watch For These Upcoming New Releases…

Coming Soon

A SNITCH ON TIME

THE MACOS ADVENTURE II THE AUTHORITY SQUAD

RUDE BUAY ... RETURNS

A SNITCH ON TIME

New Releases…

RENEGADE COPS –

A SNITCH ON TIME

CROSS ATLANTIC FIASCO

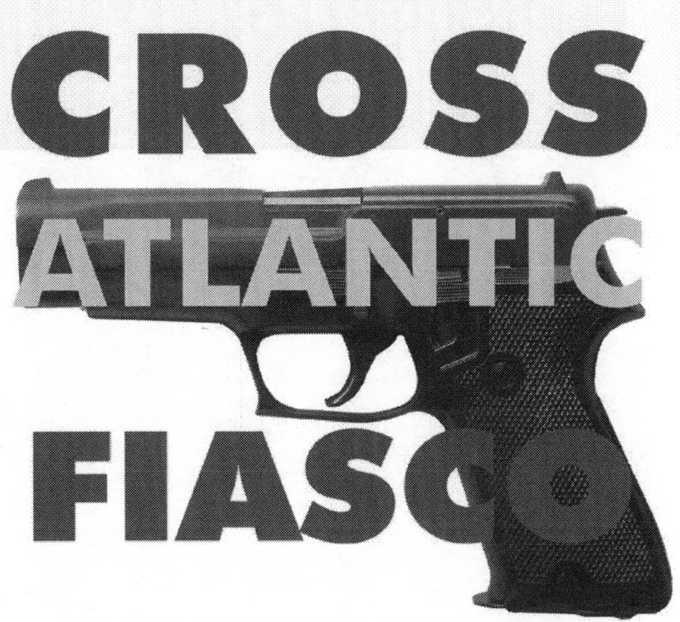

BLOOD IS THICKER THAN WATER

JOHN A. ANDREWS

RENEGADE COPS

Creator of

The RUDE BUAY Series

&

The WHODUNIT CHRONICLES

RUDE BUAY ... SHATTERPROOF

A SNITCH ON TIME

WHO SHOT THE SHERRIFF?

A SNITCH ON TIME

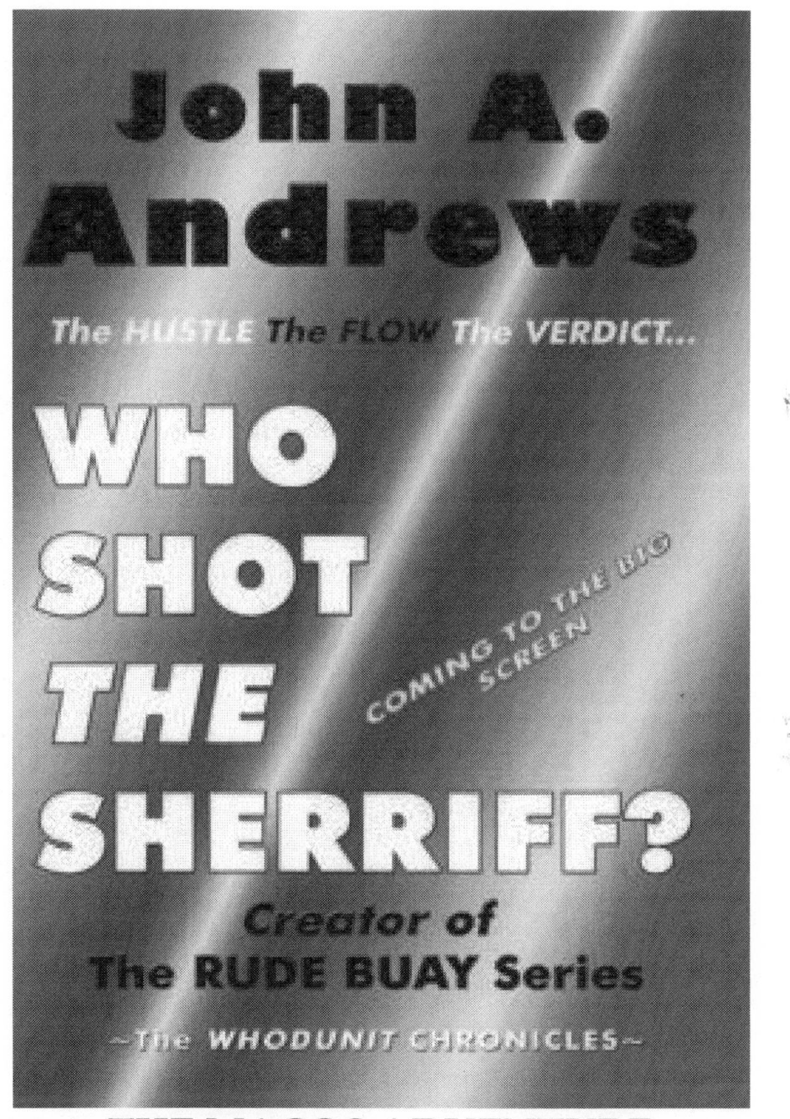

THE MACOS ADVENTURE

A SNITCH ON TIME

Other Favorites

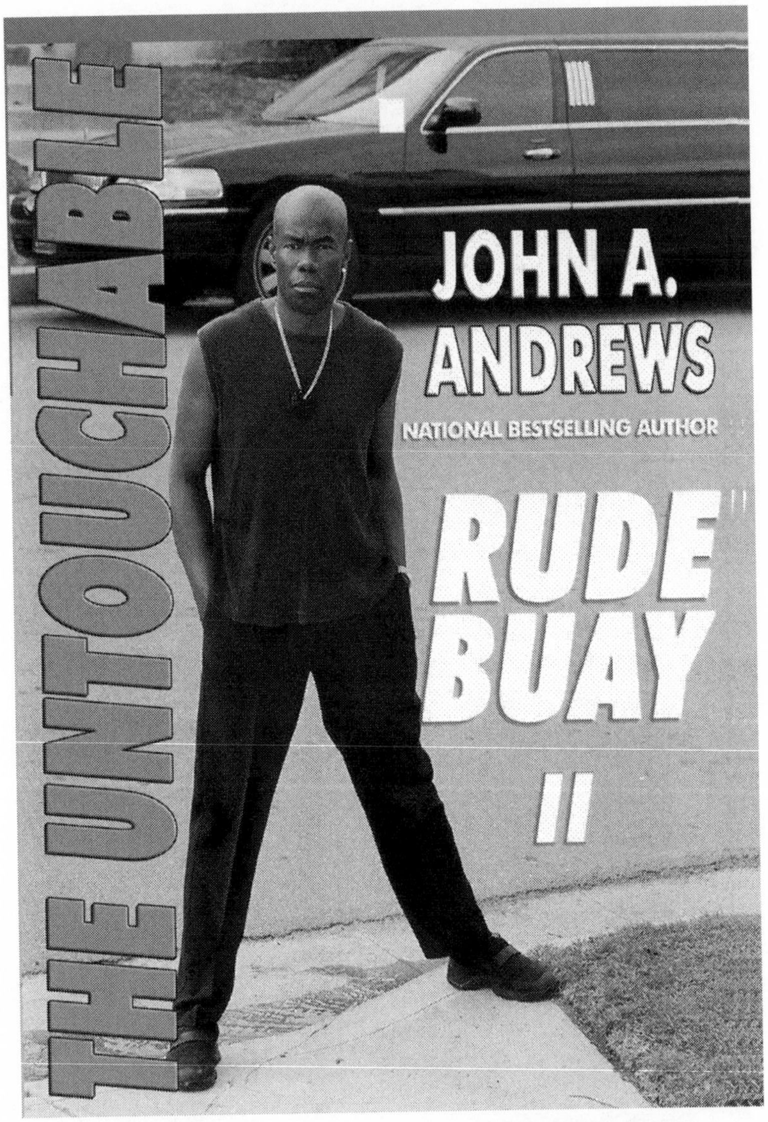

CHICO RUDO ... El INTOCABLE

A SNITCH ON TIME

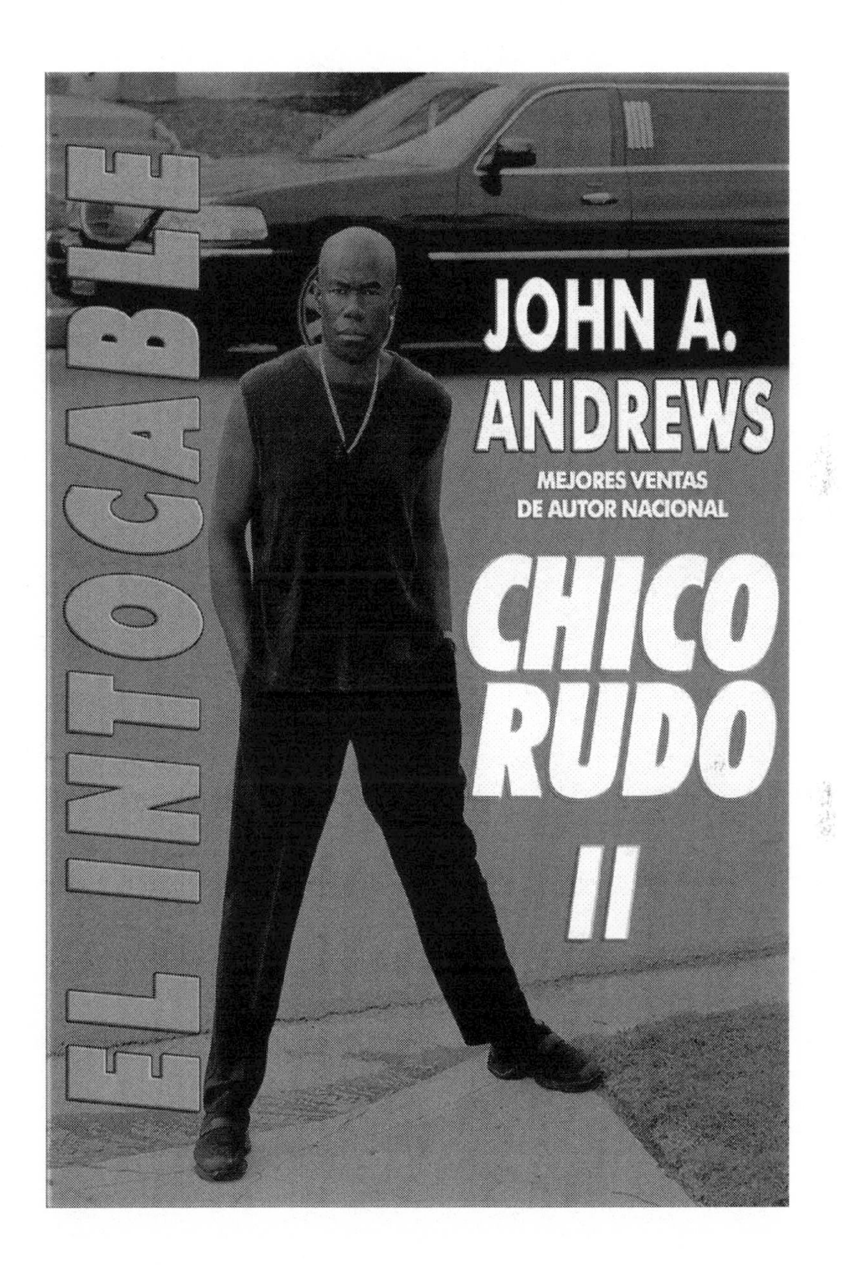

HOW I RAISED MYSELF FROM FAILURE TO SUCCESS IN HOLLYWOOD

A SNITCH ON TIME

HOW I WROTE 8 BOOKS IN ONE YEAR

How I Wrote 8 Books In One Year

JOHN A. ANDREWS

A

Author of

TOTAL COMMITTMENT

The Mindset Of Champions

A SNITCH ON TIME

RUDE BUAY ... THE UNSTOPPABLE

QUOTES UNLIMITED II

DARE TO MAKE A DIFFERENCE – SUCCESS 101

National Bestselling Author

Dare To Make
A
Difference

SUCCESS 101

JOHN A. ANDREWS

A SNITCH ON TIME

DARE TO MAKE A DIFFERENCE - SUCCESS 101 FOR TEENS

THE FIVE "Ps" FOR TEENS

QUOTES UNLIMITED

THE 5 STEPS TO CHANGING YOUR LIFE

SPREAD SOME LOVE – RELATIONSHIPS 101

TOTAL COMMITMENT

A SNITCH ON TIME

WHOSE WOMAN WAS SHE?

A SNITCH ON TIME

WHEN THE DUST SETTLES – I AM STILL STANDING

CHICO RUDO ... EL IMPARABLE

RUDE BUAY ... THE UNSTOPPABLE CHINESE EDITION

CUYA MUJER FUE ELLA?

BOOKS
THAT WILL
ENHANCE
YOUR
LIFE®

A SNITCH ON TIME

VISIT: WWW.JOHNAANDREWS.COM

www.facebook.com/Snitchontime

Made in the USA
Columbia, SC
06 August 2018